"I realized that I don't want to walk away from my kingdom, and if marrying a stranger is the way to keep them safe, then perhaps it's what needs to be done."

"So you plan to return to the palace and accept the marriage?"

"I've decided to return, yes." Olivia met his eyes, challenging him in the darkness. "But I can't fully commit to the marriage yet, knowing there is one last thing I have yet to experience in life.

"There is only one thing that truly matters to me. I cannot agree to an arranged marriage without allowing myself to experience one of the last things I truly have control over."

Roman's gaze was pure heat as he moistened his lips with one smooth flick of his tongue. If a simple look could make her feel this way, she needed to know what else he could make her feel. It was suddenly the only thing she wanted.

"I want my first time with a man to be on my terms, with someone who wants me just as badly as I want them."

Amanda Cinelli was raised in a large Irish/Italian family in the suburbs of Dublin, Ireland. Her love of romance was inspired after "borrowing" one of her mother's beloved Harlequin Presents novels at the age of twelve. Writing soon became a necessary outlet for her wildly overactive imagination. Now married with a daughter of her own, she splits her time between changing nappies, studying psychology and writing love stories.

Books by Amanda Cinelli

Harlequin Presents

Resisting the Sicilian Playboy
The Secret to Marrying Marchesi

Amanda Cinelli

ONE NIGHT WITH THE FORBIDDEN PRINCESS

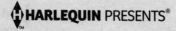

Recycling programs
for this product may
not exist in your area.

ISBN-13: 978-1-335-47800-9

One Night with the Forbidden Princess

First North American publication 2018

Copyright © 2018 by Amanda Cinelli

Printed in U.S.A.

ONE NIGHT WITH THE FORBIDDEN PRINCESS

For Zara and Mia

CHAPTER ONE

'*You will receive a marriage proposal this week.*'

Olivia's ears still rang with her father's words, even as she moved through the motions of greeting the rest of the guests at the formal luncheon. It was not every day that your father informed you that you were set to marry a stranger, after all.

But, then again, her father was a king.

And the King clearly thought that the best time to impart news of this magnitude was no less than thirty seconds before he introduced her to her intended fiancé—a complete stranger. It was a wonder that she had managed to greet their guest of honour at all before she'd hurriedly made an excuse to leave.

Princesses were generally not permitted to sneak away during royal functions. Especially when that royal function concerned a very esteemed guest of honour from a faraway kingdom. Still, Olivia found herself making her way slowly across the room in search of fresh air.

'Another glass of champagne, Your Highness?'

Olivia stopped her progress and gracefully accepted the crystal flute from the waiter's hand, noticing the way his fingers trembled slightly as he tried to balance his tray. He was quite young—fresh out of school, she would bet.

'Is this your first Royal Races?' she asked, glad of the distraction while her eyes scanned the room, plotting her escape.

'It's my first day, actually. In general,' he replied.

'You are doing a wonderful job.'

She smiled, hoping her words might help to calm his nerves somewhat. It couldn't be an easy start, balancing priceless crystal while surrounded by some of Europe's wealthiest and most famous people.

'Thank you, Princess Olivia—I mean, Your Highness. Er...thank you.' He stumbled over his words, then smiled nervously, showing a mouth full of shiny metal braces.

Olivia smiled back with genuine warmth as the boy made a wobbly attempt at a bow and moved away. She sighed, taking a small sip from her glass. She would happily have spent the rest of the afternoon chatting with the teenager simply to avoid thinking of the bombshell that had just completely taken her by surprise. As if these royal functions weren't difficult enough.

The usual array of eager guests had predictably occupied her afternoon so far, with wave after wave of polite, banal conversation. Her parents, King Fabian and Queen Aurelia of Monteverre, stood at the opposite side of the long balcony surrounded by people and bodyguards. Her own personal security team stood at strategic points around her, trying and failing to blend into the crowd in their plain black suits and crisp white shirts.

The Royal Monteverre Races were infamous around the globe for their week-long parade of upper-class style and glamour. The historic racetrack was spread out below them, and thousands of guests had gathered in their finery for a day of sport and socialising.

No one's style was more closely watched than her own. Her morning had consisted of three hours being transformed by her own personal styling team. Her naturally wavy long red hair had been ironed and pressed to perfection, and her fair skin polished and highlighted in all the right places.

The public hailed her as a stunning natural beauty, but she knew the effort that went into upholding that image was far from natural at all. She was a public brand—a symbol for an entire country with her every single step followed closely by the whole world.

Even her older sister, Crown Princess Eleanor, was not given the same amount of attention. Perhaps it was because she was already married. The press took much more pleasure in the single siblings than they did in the 'taken' ones. And yet her younger sister had the excuse of her studies in London to avoid the limelight.

For the past five years Olivia had been very much at the centre of public attention—since taking her official role in palace life at twenty-one. She did not shy from the pressure—she had been trained for it after all. She knew to expect intense scrutiny. And yet there was nothing that could make her feel more alone than being surrounded by thousands of people who treated her like an ornament to be admired from afar.

A sudden crash jolted her out of her thoughts and she looked up with a groan of empathy to see that the young waiter seemed to have lost his balance and gone crashing into a nearby couple.

'You absolute imbecile!'

The roar came from an elderly duke, a close friend of her father, who seemed to have been the sole recipient of the tray's liquid contents. Shards of priceless crystal lay scattered across the floor in a pool of expensive champagne while the teenage server stood frozen with a mixture of embarrassment and fear.

'Have this clumsy idiot taken back to the schoolroom. Out of my sight!' the Duke spat, his eyes bulging as his equally outraged wife hurriedly tried to dry his sodden shirt with a napkin.

As Olivia watched with horror, a single bodyguard materialised from the crowd and took the boy roughly by the shoulders.

'Stop!' She moved forward suddenly, her body seeming to propel her towards the dramatic scene of its own volition.

'A princess should never concern herself with such matters.'

Her late grandmother's voice seemed to warn her from her subconscious. But she pushed the thought away, arriving by the boy's side and looking up at the burly guard with all the authority she could muster. A hush had fallen over the crowd around them.

'I think there is a better way of managing this, don't you?' She addressed the guard, then turned her attention to the elderly Duke and his wife. 'Duque L'Arosa, this young man is a friend of mine. I know he would appreciate your kindness on his first day of work.'

The Duke's eyes widened horribly, his face turning even more red as his much younger wife gripped his arm and snorted her disapproval. Olivia stood her ground, flashing her best royal smile as the guard immediately released the boy. The young waiter avoided her eyes as he hurriedly gathered his tray and rushed off in the direction of the kitchen.

Olivia became suddenly painfully aware of the quiet that surrounded her. Members of the Monteverrian nobility and various public and government figures all averted their eyes, no one daring to speak or whisper about a member of the royal family while she stood in their midst.

A strange sensation began to spread over her bare shoulders, and she instinctively turned her head and found herself pinned by the gaze of a man who stood a few feet away. He was remarkably tall—taller than most of the men in the room. Perhaps that was what had drawn her attention to him.

She tried to look away, feeling uncomfortable under his obvious scrutiny, but there was something about the way he looked at her. She was quite used to being stared at—she was a public figure after all. But his dark eyes seemed to demand her complete attention. It was quite inappropriate, she told herself. She should be annoyed. But even with the length of the room between them, having his eyes on her seemed to make her heart beat faster.

A strange quiver of anticipation jolted to life in her chest, making her want to close the gap between them just to hear how his voice sounded. She raised one brow in challenge and felt her heart thump as a sinful smile spread across his full mouth, making him appear all the more rakish and infinitely dangerous.

No man had ever looked at her that way before—as though she was a tasty snack he might like to sample. She shook her head at the ridiculous turn of her thoughts and forced herself to look away.

When she finally looked back he had vanished.

She steeled her jaw, nodding politely to the Duque and Duquesa before making a slow and graceful exit through the main doors. Her own personal team of guards made themselves known as she walked faster, all five of them closing in from their previous placements. She had never felt more frustrated at her newly heightened security than she did at that moment. There was no immediate threat—no need for the ridiculous new measures her father had put in place the week before.

'I'm feeling ill,' she announced to the men once they had exited into the empty corridor outside the racetrack's function room. 'Surely there is no need for all of you to accompany me into the bathroom?'

The men reacted predictably, coughing awkwardly before moving aside and allowing her to walk unchaperoned into the ladies' restroom. She searched the for an exit point, her eyes landing on a second door on the opposite side of the bathroom. She smiled with triumph. Sometimes a little rebellion was necessary.

Roman Lazarov had never been particularly comfortable at high society functions. It had been sheer curiosity that had led him to accept the Sheikh of Zayarr's invitation to attend the Royal Races while he was already in Monteverre. Small European kingdoms were one of the few niche markets he had not yet entered with his security firm, as monarchies largely tended to keep to their own traditional models of operation. Old money aristocrats also tended to show a particular disdain towards new money Russians.

His fists tightened as he thought of the scene he had witnessed after only being in the room mere moments. Nothing made him feel closer to his own humble beginnings than watching a rich man treat his server badly. There was something particularly nasty about those who had been born to immense wealth. As though they believed the world should bend to their will and that those with less than them were somehow *worth* less as well. A sweeping generalisation, to be sure, but a painfully accurate one in his own experience.

The redhead had surprised him. She was clearly upper class—he could tell by the way she was dressed. Diamonds and rich yellow silk. He had noticed her the moment he'd entered the room. She had stood proud and untouchable near the centre, all alone, with her delicate fingers holding on to a champagne flute for dear life. And yet she had stepped forward for the servant and caused an obvious scene.

He should thank her, really. She had provided the perfect distraction for him to move on to his main purpose of business.

He would have liked nothing more than to stick around at the pretentious party and see if Lady Red lived up to his expectations. But really this brief detour to the races had been a mistake on his part. Time was of the essence when you had a royal palace to break into, after all…

The early summer afternoon was pleasant as Roman rounded the last bend on the dirt path, finally bringing the high walls of the palace into view. The overgrown abandoned hunting track wasn't the easiest route, but when you were about to break into the home of Monteverre's royal family you didn't usually use the front gate.

The forest was quiet but for the sounds of wildlife and the occasional creak of tree branches protesting as he methodically pulled them out of his way. Reaching the medieval stone wall, Roman looked up. It had to be at least five metres high and three metres thick—rather impressive and designed to be impossible to scale, especially when you weren't dressed for the occasion. He checked his smartwatch, zooming in on the small map that would guide him to the access point.

In another life Roman Lazarov had found pleasure in breaking the law. Bypassing even the most high-tech security system had been child's play for a hungry, hardened orphan with a taste for troublemaking. But in all his time in the seedy underworld of St Petersburg an actual palace had never made it onto his hit list.

That life was over now—replaced by a monumental self-made wealth that his young, hungry self could only have dreamed about. And yet here he was, his pulse quickening at the prospect of what lay ahead. The fact that this little exercise was completely above-board made it no less challenging. The palace had a guard of one hundred men and all he had was a digital blueprint of the castle tunnels and his own two hands.

The thought sent adrenaline running through his veins. God, but he had missed this feeling. When the Sheikh of Zayyar had first asked him for a favour, he had presumed it to be assembling a new security team for a foreign trip or something of that nature. Khal was in high demand these days, and his guard had been assembled almost entirely from Roman's security firm, The Lazarov Group. But Khal's request had intrigued him—likely as it had been meant to. The challenge had been set, and Roman was determined to enjoy it.

As for whether or not he would succeed—that question had made him laugh heartily in his oldest friend's face.

Roman Lazarov never failed at anything.

The daylight made it seem almost as though he were taking a leisurely stroll rather than performing an act of espionage. He finally reached the small metal hatch in the ground that would provide the cleanest and most ridiculously obvious point of entry.

An evacuation hatch, more than likely from long-ago times of war. He had hardly believed his eyes when his team had uncovered it on an old blueprint.

Although it looked rather polished and clean for a decades-old abandoned grate, he thought to himself, sliding one finger along the sun-heated metal.

A sudden sound in the quiet made Roman go completely still, instinctively holding his breath. He felt the familiar heightened awareness that came from years of experience in the security business as he listened, scanning his surroundings. Footsteps, light and fast, were coming closer. The person was of small build—possibly a child. Still, Roman couldn't be seen or this whole exercise would be blown.

Without another thought he took five long steps, shielding himself under cover of the trees.

A shape emerged from thick bushes ten feet away. The figure was petite, slim and unmistakably female. She was fast. So damned fast he saw little more than a set of bare shapely legs and a shapeless dark hooded coat before she seemed to pirouette and disappear through the hatch in the ground without any effort at all.

Roman frowned, for a moment simply replaying the image in his head. Evidently he was not the only one who had been informed of the hidden entryway. He shook off his surprise, cursing himself for hesitating as he made quick work of reaching the hatch and lowering himself.

The iron ladder was slippery with damp and led down to a smooth, square-shaped concrete tunnel beneath. Small patches of sunlight poked through ventilation ducts at regular intervals, giving some light in the otherwise pitch-blackness.

Roman stilled, listening for the sound of the woman's footsteps. She had moved quickly, but he could hear her faint steps somewhere ahead of him in the tunnel. As he began his pursuit a half-smile touched his lips. He had come here today tasked with proving the ineptitude of this palace's security, and now he would have a genuine intruder to show as proof.

This cat burglar was about to get *very* rudely interrupted.

Olivia held her shoes tightly in one hand as she slid her hand along the wall of the tunnel for support. The ground was damp and slippery under her bare feet— a fact that should have disgusted a young woman of such gentle breeding. But then she had never really understood the whole 'delicate princess' rationale. It was at times like this, after escaping palace life for even one simple hour, that she truly felt alive.

Her sudden disappearance had likely been noticed by now, and yet she did not feel any remorse. Her attendance at the international horse racing event had been aimed at the King's esteemed guest of honour,

Sheikh Khalil Al Rhas of Zayyar. The man that her father had informed her she was intended to marry.

Olivia paused for a moment, tightness overcoming her throat for the second time in a few short hours. The way he had phrased it, as her 'royal duty', still rung in her ears. She was only twenty-six, for goodness' sake. She wasn't ready for this particular duty.

She had always known it was customary for her father to hold the right to arrange or refuse the marriages of his offspring, but she had hoped the day would never come when she was called upon in such an archaic fashion. But now that day was here, and the Sheikh was set to propose to her formally any day now—before he completed his trip.

Olivia pressed her forehead briefly against the stone wall. She felt cold through and through, as if she would never be warm again.

'Drama queen.' Cressida's mocking voice sounded in her head.

Her younger sister had always been such a calm, level-headed presence in her life. It had been five years since Cress had moved away to study in England. And not a day passed that she didn't think of her. With barely a year between them, they had always been more like twins. Cress would know exactly what to say to alleviate the unbearable tension that had taken residence in her stomach today. She was sure of it.

The tunnel was a straight path along the south

boundary of the palace. It seemed like an endless mile before the staircase finally appeared. Olivia climbed it in the near darkness, relying solely on memory to make her way up to the partially hidden door in the stone wall. She pressed a slim crease, sliding open a panel and stepping through easily.

The brightness of her dressing room was a welcome shock of cream and gold after the prolonged darkness. She took a moment, breathing in the clean air, before turning to slide the secret door closed.

Olivia stilled at the sound of footsteps in the tunnel below. But that was impossible. In almost fifteen years of roaming she had never seen another soul down there. She had never even told her sisters.

She stepped back down to the small landing at the top of the steps. She braced her hands on the stone balustrade to peer down into the darkness, biting the inside of her lip. Had one of the guards followed her?

The footsteps suddenly disappeared and an eerie silence filled the stone caverns. Still she held her breath. *Eight, nine, ten...* Olivia exhaled slowly, cursing her overactive imagination. The silence of the tunnel tended to play with your mind after a while—she was clearly going insane.

She turned around to move back to the doorway to her apartment—only to be blocked by a wall of muscle. Warm muscle that smelled of sandalwood and pine.

Strong hands—definitely male—appeared like

chains across her chest and turned her towards the wall. Her arms were pulled behind her and she instinctively pushed her body backwards, aiming the hardness of her skull towards her assailant's nose. Even princesses were taught self-defence.

'You have some skills, I see.'

His voice was startling in the quiet darkness. A heavy accent made his threat even more worrying. This was most definitely *not* a palace guard.

Olivia hissed, turning away and trying in vain to pull against the bands of iron strength. She squinted in the darkness, trying to see his face, a uniform, an insignia—anything that might tell her who he was and why he was here. If she could remember anything from the Palace Guards' kidnapping talk it was one thing: *Don't say a thing.*

He pressed on what seemed to be a watch and turned a faint light downwards, lowering its beam to her oversized black trench coat and bare feet. She had swapped her designer blazer with someone else's coat in the cloakroom before bolting. The vintage lemon cocktail dress she wore underneath was hardly ideal for going unnoticed in public.

She turned her head and caught a brief glimpse of a hard jaw and gigantic shoulders before he plunged them into darkness once more.

'You're not exactly dressed for a quick escape,' he mused.

She almost laughed at that—almost. But being

held captive by a mysterious hulk of a man had kind of dampened her infamous ability to see the bright side of every situation. As far as she could see there was nothing positive that could come of being abducted, which was the only logical solution for whoever this man was. He would recognise her any moment now and the game would be up.

Perhaps they would ransom her, she thought wildly. How much was her life worth? Hopefully not too much…the kingdom was already facing complete financial ruin as it was.

She gulped hard as she felt his hand slip just under her left armpit—a strange place to grope, indeed.

'Don't! Don't you dare touch me.' She gasped, arching her body away frantically. He tightened his hold on her slightly, barely even noticing her attempts to free herself.

'You are in no danger from me,' he gritted. 'I must ensure the same can be said of you. Stand still.'

Such was the authority in his voice that she stilled herself. She held her breath as his touch moved almost mechanically to her hip. His movements were calm and purposeful as he did the same to her other side, feeling inside the pockets of her coat and underneath to slide along the indentation of her waist.

Her mind suddenly realised that he was searching for a weapon. She sucked in a breath as strong fingers brushed her ribcage, just underneath her breasts. Of all the situations in which to become excited by a man's touch, this really wasn't it. And yet her traitorous body had begun to respond to the intensity of the situation even as her heart thumped with fear.

His breathing did not alter at all, and nor did he show any signs of noticing her response. As his hand finally moved to her thigh Olivia could take no more. She kicked out. Partly in shock at his boldness, but mostly because of the discomfort of her own reaction.

She took a deep breath. 'Do you honestly believe that I'm hiding a weapon in my underwear?'

The stranger cleared his throat. 'I have known people to hide weapons in the most ludicrous places. Women especially tend towards a certain…creativity.'

'Do *not* put your hands on me again.'

He was silent for a moment, and the only sound in the dark tunnel was that of their steady breaths mingling in the air between them.

When he spoke again his accent was more pronounced, his voice deep and intimidating. 'Tell me who you are and why you are attempting to break into the palace.'

She paused at that. So he hadn't recognised her yet. Surely if he was a kidnapper he would have come here knowing the faces of the royal family. Although it was dark, she supposed. Her choices were limited. She had no panic buttons down here—no guards within shouting distance.

She needed to get away.

She turned her head towards the door, breathing a little faster with anticipation as his shrewd gaze followed the movement and he saw the sliver of light coming through the gap.

'You managed to find a way inside, I see,' he said with surprise. 'Come on, then. Let's see what you were after, shall we?'

He held her forearm tightly, dragging her behind him up the steps and into the lavish dressing room. Her eyes adjusted quickly once again, to take in the rows and rows of her wardrobes. The room was empty, as it would be for a while, seeing as her staff presumed her to be at the races for the rest of the day.

Olivia gulped hard. She had just led an uncleared intruder right into the heart of the palace.

She took a moment to look at him for the first time in the light.

'It's you…' she breathed, realising it was the man from the racetrack.

To his credit, he also looked momentarily stunned as he took in her face in the light.

He was taller this close—almost an entire foot taller than her five feet three inches. All the self-defence classes in the world wouldn't give her a hope against such a brute. Dark hair, dark eyes and a jawline that would put Michelangelo's *David* to shame. He had a fierce beauty about him—as if he had just stepped off a battlefield somewhere—and he thrummed with vitality.

Her grandmother had always said she watched too many movies. Here she was, in very real danger, and she was romanticising her captor.

'You have taken a break from saving servants, I see.' His eyes lowered to take in the coat that covered her cocktail dress. 'You seem to be a woman of many talents.'

Olivia stayed completely silent as he spoke, knowing the more she said the more chance there was that he would put two and two together and guess her identity. She glanced to her left, searching the room for possible weapons for when the time came to run. If she could find something to kick at him, perhaps...

She looked down at her bare feet, cursing her own stupidity.

'We are in the south wing,' he mused, looking around the room. 'One of the royal apartments. How did you find out about the hidden tunnel?'

She shrugged, looking down at her feet and taking one tentative step away from him while his attention wandered.

'I saw how you slid down there. You knew exactly what you were doing. Just like you know what you are doing right now.' He grabbed her arm, stopping her progress.

She couldn't help herself then—she cursed. A

filthy word in Catalan that would make her father blush if he heard her.

The stranger smiled darkly. 'We're going to get absolutely nowhere if you don't speak to me. Why are you here?' he asked again, releasing her arm and pushing her to sit down in the chair in front of her dressing table.

Exactly where she needed to be.

'I could ask you the same question,' she replied, slowly reclining backwards under the pretext of stretching her tender muscles.

'That's simple. I'm here for people like you,' he said simply, crossing his arms and staring down at her.

'People like me?' she asked breathlessly, her hand feeling blindly along the dressing table behind her for where she knew an alert button had been placed. She tried to calm her breath and prayed he would not see what she was doing. She felt a smooth round bump and pressed it quickly, holding her breath in case she needed to run.

No sirens sounded…there were no flashing lights. She moved to press it again, only to have his fingers encircle her elbow and place her hands in her lap.

'Keep your hands where I can see them.'

It was clear this wasn't going to be over any time soon.

He tilted his head to one side, looking at her in such an intense way it made her toes curl into the carpet under her feet. His eyes lowered, darkening as they swept down her legs.

The way he looked at her, the blatant male appreciation on his striking features, made something seem to uncoil in the pit of her stomach. She felt warm under his gaze and turned her face away in case she blushed.

'Whomever you think I am, I can tell you now that you are very wrong.'

His answering smile was raking, and made goosebumps break out across her arms.

The stranger bent down so that their faces were level. 'I think that, whoever you are, beautiful, you are a lot stronger and a lot more dangerous than you seem.'

CHAPTER TWO

'YOU SOUND LIKE quite the expert,' she purred, her catlike eyes seeming to glow in her pale features.

Roman frowned. 'I can tell by your eyes that you're worried about being caught in the act, and yet you mock me.'

'You're quite arrogant and you deserve some mocking, I think,' she replied sweetly.

He fought the urge to laugh at this situation. Here he was, with a thief held captive inside the palace walls, and he was enjoying their verbal sparring too much to make a decision over what to do with her.

He couldn't simply waltz up to the King's offices and present him with this gift. Problem one being that the King was out of the palace today, along with the rest of the royal family. Problem two being that the Palace Guard had no idea he would be here today. As far as they were concerned he would be just as much a criminal as the sharp-tongued redhead who sat staring at him as though she'd like to claw his eyes out.

He would have to call Khal and tell him that their plan had encountered a minor diversion. It was no matter, really. He had identified a serious security blind spot and provided the Palace Guard with an attempted burglar to boot. All in all, quite a success.

So why did the thought of handing her over make him feel so uneasy?

He had got where he was by trusting his gut, and right now his gut was telling him that something wasn't quite right here. That this woman was not all that she seemed. Something made him pause, his brain weighing the situation up piece by piece.

'You are quite possibly the most ladylike thief I have ever encountered,' he mused. 'Do you always go barefoot on a job, or was today an exception?'

'You assume that I make a habit of this?' She glared up at him.

'Correct me, then.' He held her gaze evenly until she looked away.

'You have quite an intense stare. It's making me uneasy.'

She crossed one slim leg over the other. Roman felt his throat go dry, and looked away from the expanse of creamy smooth skin below her dress.

'I'm in the business of being observant,' he said, clearing his throat. 'You might benefit from it yourself, then maybe next time you won't get caught so easily.'

'I assume you are the almighty authority on how

to break into palaces?' She raised her brows, sitting straighter in her seat.

'Seeing as you arrived here first, I disagree,' he countered.

'Oh, *now* I see. You're angry that you were beaten to the punch by a woman.' She placed both feet flat on the floor, smoothing her dress over her knees. 'This whole body-searching, intimidating act has all been one big ego-stroke for you.'

'I searched you because I am not so pig-headed as to believe that you pose no threat to me simply because of your sex.' Roman shook his head in disbelief, hating himself for rising to her bait. 'Why would you assume that the fact you are a woman has anything to do with it?'

She looked away from him then. 'Because it always does.'

'I think that's far more telling of your low opinion of men than anything else.' He raised his brows. 'Trust me, I am an expert in assessing risks. Women are not somehow physically destined to surrender to men. I have seen it first-hand. I have trained women, watched them down men twice their size without breaking a sweat.'

'You *train* women? To become…thieves?' she said with disbelief. 'Who on earth *are* you?'

Roman laughed, not bothering to correct her assumption. 'Let's just say I am the last person you wish to meet while you're on a job. Not just here, in this castle. Anywhere. I know how the criminal mind works. I have made it my business to be an expert in it.'

'So if I'm a criminal, you'll know what I am thinking right now?' Her eyes darted towards the door once more.

'I'm trying to.' Roman poised himself in case she ran. 'Just tell me what it is you're after and I can make this easier for you. Tell me your name.'

'No,' she said plainly.

Her body language was telling him that she was becoming increasingly more agitated with the situation. A flight risk if ever he'd seen one.

Even as the thought crossed his mind she jumped from the chair, her speed surprising him for a split second before he moved himself. She made it a few steps before his arms were around her waist, holding her body tightly against his as she struggled in vain.

'Please—just let me go,' she breathed.

The fear in her voice startled him, but his training had taught him not to release anyone until he had another means of restraining them.

'You are making it very difficult for me to help you here. Do you know that?' he said, holding her arms tightly to her sides and trying in vain to ignore the delicious scent of vanilla that drifted up from her hair.

'Why…? Why would you offer to help after what you think of me?'

He thought for a moment. 'Because I believe in second chances.' He spoke without thought, his answer surprising even himself. 'You always have a choice—no matter how impossible it seems.'

A strange look came over her face as their eyes locked. Her breath was coming hard and heavy against his chest but she'd stopped fighting him. Her eyes drifted away from him, settling on the distance with a mixture of resolve and deep sadness.

'I'm not who you think I am.'

Without warning a heavy weight came down behind him, followed by what he presumed to be a palace guard shouting in furious Catalan.

Roman pushed the man backwards, holding his hands up in what he hoped resembled a peaceful motion.

'I have authorisation,' he began, motioning towards the lapel of his suit jacket. 'The King knows I am here.'

Roman felt his hands being pulled behind him into handcuffs and fought the urge to laugh as he looked up into a second guard's furious face.

'You will regret this.'

He grunted at the pressure of a knee between his shoulder blades, knowing that they most likely did not speak a word of English. As his face was crushed against the carpet he looked sideways, just in time to see a pair of dainty bare feet appear by his side. Up close, he could see that a tiny hand-drawn daisy adorned each red-painted toenail.

The woman spoke in rapid-fire Catalan, her voice muted and fearful yet with a strange backbone of authority. The nearest guard nodded, uttering two words that made his body freeze.

'Si, Princesa.'

Roman crushed his face further into the carpet with disbelief and sheer dread.

He had just body-searched a damn princess.

His Majesty King Fabian of Monteverre stood up as Olivia entered the private sitting room flanked by two stony-faced members of the Royal Guard.

'Of all the days to pull one of your disappearing acts, Libby,' her father said angrily, motioning for the guards to leave them with a flick of one hand.

Her mother, elegant and perpetually silent, did not acknowledge her entry. Queen Aurelia sat poised in a high-backed chair, her eyes trained solemnly on nothing in particular.

'Where have you *been*? You were informed of the intruder hours ago,' Olivia said, breathing hard.

'And naturally you expected us to abandon the event? Honestly, Libby…' The King frowned in disbelief, reaching down to take a sip of whisky from a thick crystal tumbler.

Her father was the only one who still called her

Libby. It reminded her of being five years old and being scolded for trying to sneak chocolate from the kitchens. But she was not a child any more, and she was damned tired of being treated like one.

'I was attacked,' she said slowly. 'A man held me hostage in my own dressing room. And yet I've been left to pace my apartments completely alone for the past five hours.'

'The matter has been resolved. It was a simple misunderstanding.' King Fabian avoided his daughter's eyes. 'Best to forget the whole business.'

Olivia felt all the outrage and pent-up frustration freeze in her veins as she registered her father's words. Had he actually just told her to *forget* this afternoon? She opened her mouth, then closed it, completely at a loss as to what to say in response.

'Your absence was noticed by Sheikh Khalil,' he said, scolding, his brows drawing down as they always did when he was unimpressed.

'Well, as I have just said, I was rather busy being held against my will by a dangerous intruder.' She took a deep breath, looking briefly across to her mother's uninterested blank features before returning her furious gaze to her father. 'Have I gone mad? Or are you both completely unaffected by today's events?'

'I understand it might have been…alarming…' King Fabian began solemnly.

'"Alarming" hardly covers it.' Olivia fumed. 'Why are you both so *calm*?'

The last word came out in a disbelieving whisper. She fought a distinct urge to walk over and bang her fist on her father's chest, to knock over her mother's glass, to make them both react in some way other than with this muted nothingness.

Today's events had shaken her to her core, and yet she felt as though she were intruding on their peace with her inconvenient outrage. Surely her own father should be shocked and outraged that his daughter's safety had been at risk inside their own home. Unless... Unless he wasn't shocked at all.

'What do you mean by a misunderstanding?' she asked, not bothering to hide the challenge in her voice.

'Libby...' Her father sighed, raising a hand for her to quieten.

'Please, don't "Libby" me.' She placed one hand on her hip. 'Tell me exactly what is going on. Did you know about this man?'

The King twisted his mouth in discomfort. 'Well...not directly, no.'

'Indirectly, then. You *knew* that someone would be here today? In our home.'

King Fabian strode to the window, placing one hand on the sill and looking out in silence. 'The man you met today was Roman Lazarov, founder of The Lazarov Group, an international security firm.' Her father sighed heavily. 'He is a very close friend of Sheikh Khalil and I have been assured that he is *the* authority on high-class security operations. But after the complete muddle he made today, I'm not so sure of his expert status…'

He laughed weakly, his voice trailing off as he took in her expression of horror.

'Don't look at me that way. It was a gift from Sheikh Khalil—very thoughtful of him to want to ensure your safety, I thought.'

Olivia felt a headache begin at her temples. This was all becoming too much. She closed her eyes a moment, unable to bear her father's apparent disregard for his daughter's privacy or independence.

'No, Father. In fact I find it horribly thoughtless. And intrusive, among other things.' She felt her breath coming faster, her temper rising like a caged bird set to take flight. 'This is the last straw in a long line of things I have overlooked since you began vaguely mentioning a possible marriage. I am not a piece of livestock to be insured and fenced in, for goodness' sake.'

He sighed. 'You are overreacting.'

'No, I'm really not. Did anyone consult me before all my charity events were cancelled? Was I informed when I was assigned five new bodyguards for all trips outside the palace?' She shook her head, her knuckles straining with the tightness of her fists by her sides. 'And now this. Did you even think to ask me before you sent a bloody *mercenary* into my room? I'll never feel safe there again!'

'Lazarov was simply going to *attempt* to gain entry to your rooms. To find any weaknesses in our security. Besides, you were supposed to be at the races with your fiancé.'

The tightness in her throat intensified. 'I have not yet agreed to this marriage. Until today I had no idea that you were truly serious about it! And if this is how the Sheikh shows his concern…'

She tightened her lips, willing herself to say the words. To tell her father that the whole deal was off. She didn't want this. *Any* of it.

King Fabian's voice lowered in warning. 'Olivia, these negotiations are months old—we have discussed why this is a necessary step.'

She blinked. *Months old?* 'For the kingdom, yes. I understand what we stand to gain from a political union.' She cleared her throat, her voice sounding all of a sudden smaller. 'But what about for *me*?'

Her father's brows rose imperiously. 'You will be serving your kingdom.'

'I don't see why I must get married to a complete stranger in order to serve Monteverre. I am doing good work with Mimi's Foundation—I am making a difference.'

'Your grandmother and her damned charities…' Fabian scowled darkly, draining the last of his whisky. 'You think teaching a handful of scrawny kids to read will change anything about our situation?'

'My grandmother taught me that charity is not always about money. It's important to nourish the youth as well as to do our best to help those in need. She was beloved by this kingdom.'

'Ah, yes, the eternally perfect Queen Miranda! My mother spent so much time on her charities she didn't even notice her country's economy crumbling beneath her feet.' His mouth twisted cruelly. 'Don't you *see*, you silly girl? We are facing financial ruin without this union.'

Olivia opened her mouth to protest, only to have her father's scowl stop her as he continued on his own personal rant.

'The Kingdom of Zayyar is overflowing with wealth, thanks to this man. He is an economic genius. But the civic history of his country still stands in the way of true acceptance from the west. To put it bluntly, they need our political influence and we need their money.'

'Money...' Olivia bit her lip, wanting to ask just how much she was worth, considering he was essentially trading her body for cash.

'Sheikh Khalil has the capabilities to take Monteverre back to its glory days—surely you want that for your people? What good is being able to read if they have no money to feed themselves?'

She had never heard her father speak so frankly, and his eyes were red-rimmed with half-madness. Olivia knew that Monteverre was in trouble. A series of bad leadership decisions and banking crashes had left them neck-deep in debt and with many of the younger generation emigrating to greener pastures. They were bleeding, and it appeared that this Sheikh had come offering a magic bandage. At a particular cost...

'Trusting an entire country's economic future to one man's hands? That seems a bit...reckless. Surely there is another way without the marriage—?'

'No,' he cut across her, his voice a dull bark in the silent room. 'There is no going back on this. I won't hear another word.'

Her father's eyes were dark in a way she had never seen them before, as though he hadn't truly slept in months.

'Everything you have had since birth is thanks to your position. It's not like you have an actual *career* to think of—you spend most of your time looking pretty and waving. None of that would even change. Your life would continue just as it has been—only as the Sheikha of Zayyar.' He took a breath, smiling down at her as if he had just bestowed upon her some enormous gift. 'This is your *duty*, Olivia. To Monteverre. It's not about you.'

She felt his words sink into her skin like an icy breeze, setting off goose pimples down her bare arms. Did being born a Sandoval really mean surrendering every aspect of your life to the good of the kingdom?

As the second daughter she had naïvely believed that her life would be different from her older sister's. She was not first in line to rule Monteverre—she didn't bear that crushing weight of responsibility and she had always been infinitely glad of it.

'The Sheikha of Zayyar...'

Her mother's melodic voice intruded on her thoughts, sounding absurdly serene.

'Sounds like something from a film...'

'I don't even know where Zayyar is,' Olivia said numbly, almost unable to speak past the tickle of panic spreading across her throat.

'Somewhere on the Persian Gulf,' Queen Aurelia offered, twirling the liquid in her glass. 'They have a hotel shaped like a boat sail.'

'That's Dubai.' King Fabian rolled his eyes. 'Zayyar is halfway between the desert and the Arabian Sea. Gorgeous scenery—you will love it.'

'Thank you for the sales pitch, Father.' Olivia sighed, looking across to her mother, who had once again turned to gaze into the empty fireplace.

It was customary for her mother to permanently nurse a glass of the finest cognac after midday. In Olivia's memory no one had ever questioned it or raised any concern. There had always been an unspoken understanding among the Sandoval children that their mother and father each did whatever they pleased and things would always be that way. They did not welcome personal discussions.

She looked up to the ceiling, feeling the familiar sense of exhaustion that always accompanied any meeting with her parents. For that was all they ever were. Meetings.

'Sheikh Khalil simply wanted to ensure your safety, Libby. Surely you find that romantic? I know you are prone to the sentiment.'

Her father looked down at his wife, but she had drifted off, her eyes dull and unfocused as she stared into nothingness. The look on his face changed to outright disgust and he turned away, busying himself with retrieving his jacket from a chair.

Olivia's heart broke a little for her parents' fractured marriage. She had fleeting memories of a happier time, when her parents had seemed madly in love and the Kingdom of Monteverre had been a shining beacon of prosperity and culture. Now there was nothing but cold resentment and constant worry.

'Father...' Olivia took a breath, trying to calm her rapid thoughts. 'This is all happening very fast. Perhaps if I just had some more time—'

'Why do you think the Sheikh arranged this trip? He plans to propose formally this afternoon so that the announcement can be made public before he leaves.'

Olivia's breath caught, expanding her throat painfully. 'He...he can't do that...'

'Oh, yes, he can—and you will be grateful for his patience.'

His voice boomed across the room, the sudden anger in it startling her, making her back away a step.

He took a breath, deliberately softening his tone. 'Can't you see that you are a vital part in this? There is power in your position.'

'Power...' Olivia repeated weakly. Her shoulders drooped. Even her bones felt heavy. *Women are not always destined to surrender to men...* Those words—*his* words—had struck something deep within her.

Roman Lazarov.

She bit her lip hard. For a moment she had regretted her decision to have him captured. He had seemed to glow from within—a fiery protector and proclaimer of women's strength. Now she knew he was just like the rest of them. Here to ensure that her cage was kept good and tight. That she had no hope of freedom.

King Fabian tightened his lips, forcing a smile before shrugging into his navy dress jacket and fixing the diamond cufflinks at his wrists. He paused by her side, looking down at her.

'You will have a private lunch with Sheikh Khalil tomorrow.' He placed one hand on her shoulder, giving it a light squeeze. 'I know you will give him the answer he wants. I'm so proud of the beautiful woman you have become.'

Olivia closed her eyes, not wanting him to see the tears that glistened there. Her heart seemed to slow in her chest as she nodded her head in defeat, glad when he was gone, with the smell of cigar smoke wafting on the air in his wake. How could he be proud of the woman she was when she had no idea who she was herself?

'I can't do this,' she breathed, silently hoping her mother would look up. That she would hold her and listen to her worries, then kiss her forehead and tell her everything would be okay.

But sadly she knew that would never happen. She had no memories of ever being in her mother's arms, and even if she had the woman who now sat like a living ghost in the sitting room was not truly her mother.

She stood still for a long time, letting the tears fall down her cheeks and stain the neckline of her dress. Eventually she wiped her face and turned away from the unbearable silence, walking through the long main corridors of the private suites.

As usual, the guards pretended not to notice her.

She took her time, idling through the gardens on her way back to her rooms. With a few deep breaths she calmed the tremor in her throat. It had been a long time since she had let a single tear fall—probably not since the day of her grandmother's funeral. Crying was a fruitless activity when her future had already been neatly packed up and arranged.

She sat heavily on a marble bench in the centre of the courtyard. This was her favourite part of the palace, where a low stone square fountain provided the perfect vantage point to sit and listen to the staff as they went about their daily duties. Here, partially concealed by bougainvillea and foliage, she had been privy to the most heart-stopping live-action dramas outside of television.

The fights, the wicked gossip, the passionate clandestine embraces. A reluctant smile touched her lips. She had seen it all.

Just in the past month it had been revealed that one of the upstairs maids had engaged in an affair with the head gardener's handsome son. Olivia had overheard the whole sordid situation developing— right up to the point when said housemaid had found out that her beau was also heavily involved with one of the palace florists. The ensuing slap had resounded across the courtyard and earned the young Romeo a speedy transfer outside the palace.

The housemaid had moved on quickly enough, accepting a date with a palace guard. The look of delirious happiness as she'd described their first kiss to her friends had haunted Olivia for days.

She stood restlessly, leaning against the side of the fountain. Was that look the very thing she was sacrificing by agreeing to a loveless marriage?

She frowned, drawing her hand through the water and watching the ripples spread across her own solemn reflection. Love was about falling for the wrong guy, having your heart broken and then ending up with your handsome Prince Charming—not that she had ever experienced it. But she had watched enough old movies to know it was always true love's kiss at the end that gave her that butterflies feeling in her stomach. That moment when the couple swore their undying devotion and fell into each other's arms...

She wanted to feel like that. At least once in her life.

There had been a handful of kisses in her past; she was twenty-six, after all. But never more than a brief touching of lips. The kind of men who had been permitted near her just happened to be the kind of men who got aroused at the thought of their own reputations inflating with a real-life princess on their arm. Not one of the men she'd dated had ever tried to get to know her *really*.

A prickle made its way along her skin as she thought of a certain pair of grey eyes, raking their way down her body. It was madness, the way her body had seemed to thrum deep inside just from a man's gaze. It was ridiculous.

She looked down at her forearms, seeing the gooseflesh there. Why did he have to affect her so violently when no other man had managed to inspire so much as a flicker of her attraction?

She bit the inside of her cheek with frustration and

turned to begin walking back to her apartments—
only to find a large male frame blocking her path.

'Good evening, Printsessa.'

CHAPTER THREE

'I SEE THEY have released you... Mr Lazarov.' The Princess straightened her shoulders defensively, moving a long silken curtain of vibrant red hair away from her face as she directed her gaze upon him.

Roman ignored the strange tightening in his stomach at the way she said his name, focusing on her pale features to better read her mood.

She seemed less colourful than he remembered—as if something had stolen the fire he had witnessed earlier in the day, both at the racetrack and afterwards.

'Once they realised their mistake they were quite accommodating. I hope you were not worried for my welfare.'

'If it were my choice I would have had you detained for the night.'

She held her chin high as she delivered the blow, but Roman saw the telltale convulsive movement in her throat as she took a breath. He leaned casually against a nearby column, raising a single brow in challenge.

Far from bowing under his scrutiny, she held his gaze evenly. 'I assume you are here to make your apology?'

Roman fought the urge to laugh. 'I'm no stranger to handcuffs, Princess.' He smiled darkly. 'It would take more than five hours in a cushy palace detainment room to force me to my knees.'

Her gaze lowered a fraction and Roman gave in to his mirth, a darkly amused smile spreading across his lips.

'I don't want you to be on your...' She shook her head, exhaling hard. She crossed her arms below her chest—a gesture likely meant in defence, but all it served to do was draw his attention to the resulting swell at the neckline of her delicate yellow dress.

'Well, you are free to go,' she said, sarcasm dripping from her tone as she gestured towards the door to the main palace.

For the first time in his life Roman was at a complete loss as to what to say. How he had not recognised that she was a royal instantly, he did not know. The woman before him seemed to exude class and sophistication in every inch of her posture. She eyed him with suspicion, her brows lowering in a mixture of challenge and defence.

He should have left the moment he had been freed, and yet he had sought her out. He had told himself he needed to apologise, but right now, remembering the honest arousal in her eyes as he'd been pressed close to her... He wasn't feeling quite so apologetic.

He stood taller, hardening his voice. 'In case you are planning another escape, the tunnel has been blocked. It is no longer passable.'

'You certainly work fast,' she said quietly, leaning back against the lip of the fountain. 'I assume the Sheikh asked you to make sure my cage was good and tight?'

'Your...cage?'

She was oblivious to his confusion. 'Of course it matters to no one that I am an adult with free will. By all means let him have the run of the palace. There will be bars installed on my bedroom windows next.'

Roman raked a hand across the shadow beginning to grow along his jaw. He allowed her to a rant a moment, before clearing his throat pointedly. 'You seem upset.'

'"Upset" does not even begin to cover it. Everything about today has been unbearable.'

Something about the faraway look in her eyes bothered him. It was as though she were on the edge of a complete meltdown, and he worried that it was his mistake that had brought her there. Perhaps there was a need for his apology after all—much as it pained him to admit it.

'Princess, I need you to understand that I am not

in the habit of holding a woman against her will,' he said solemnly. 'Earlier...when I searched you...'

She looked back at him, her lashes half lowered with something dark and unspoken. 'Will you be telling your fearsome Sheikh about that, I wonder?'

'The Sheikh is not the villain you seem to think he is,' Roman said quietly, inwardly grimacing at the thought of telling his best friend how he had man-handled his future wife. 'I have never known some-one as loyal and dedicated.'

'Perhaps the two of you should get married, then,' she said snidely.

'I did not expect an actual princess to be quite so...cutting.' He pressed a hand to his chest in mock injury. 'Is it any wonder I mistook you for a com-mon thief?'

That earned him the hint of a smile from her lips. The movement lit up her eyes ever so slightly and he felt a little triumphant that he had caused it.

Roman smirked, turning to lean against the foun-tain, taking care to leave a good foot and a half of space between them. It had been a long time since he had been this conscious of a woman's presence.

'You seem like quite the man of mystery, Mr Laz-arov,' she said, turning to look at him briefly. 'Best friends with a sheikh...founder of an international security firm.'

'You've been researching me?'

'I only found out your name twenty minutes ago,'

she said honestly. 'Does the Sheikh always fly you in for such favours?'

'No, he does not.' Roman felt the corner of his mouth tilt at her mocking. It had been a long time since a woman had been so obviously unimpressed by him. 'I have my own means of transportation for such occasions.'

'Let me guess—something small and powerful with tinted windows?'

'It is black.' His lips twisted with amusement at her jibe. 'But my yacht is hardly small. No tinted windows—I much prefer the light.'

Her gaze wandered, the smile fading from her lips as she looked away from him. 'A playboy's yacht... of course.'

'These things have not magically fallen into my lap, I assure you. I have worked hard for the life-style I enjoy.'

'Oh, I didn't mean...' She turned her face back towards him quickly. 'I envy you, that's all.'

He raised a brow, wondering not for the first time what on earth was going on inside her head. 'There is an entire fleet of vessels moored in the harbour with the royal crest on their hulls. You're telling me you couldn't just choose one at will?'

'I spent years learning how to sail at school. But I have yet to go on a single trip by myself,' she said, looking up and meeting his eyes for a long moment. 'It's strange...' she began, before shaking her head and turning her face away. 'I've spoken more frankly with you today—a complete stranger—than I have with anyone in a long time.'

Roman did not know how to respond to that statement. He swallowed hard, looking ahead to where a group of housemaids walked and chatted their way across the second-floor balconies. When he finally looked back the Princess had moved from beside him.

He stood up, looking around him for a sign of where she had gone, only to see a glimpse of pale yellow silk disappearing through the archway that led to the royal apartments.

He took a step forward, then caught himself.

She was where she belonged—surrounded by guards and staff.

It was time for him to get back to his own life.

The afternoon sun was hot on his neck when Roman finally walked out onto the deck of his yacht the next day. In his line of work he was no stranger to going to sleep as the sun rose, but his restless night had little to do with work. Being handcuffed in a room by himself had given him far too much time with his own thoughts. A dangerous pastime for a man with a past like his.

Nursing a strong black coffee, he slid on dark sunglasses and sank down into a hammock chair. They would set sail for the *isla* soon enough, and he would be glad to see the back of this kingdom and all its upper-class pomp.

He surveyed the busy harbour of Puerto Reina, Monteverre's main port. Tourists and locals peppered the busy marble promenade that fronted the harbour—the Queen's Balcony, he had been told it was called. A glittering golden crown insignia was emblazoned over every sign in the town, as though the people might somehow otherwise forget that it was the crown that held the power.

Never had he met a man more blinded by his own power than His Majesty, King Fabian. Khal had insisted on them meeting two nights previously, so that the three men could discuss the situation of the Princess's security—Khal was notoriously meticulous when it came to bodyguards and security measures.

It had been clear from the outset that Roman would be treated like the commoner he was, so he had made the choice to leave, rather than sit and be spoken down to. His tolerance levels only stretched so far. It seemed His Majesty still harboured some ill will, as made apparent by the gap of five hours between the time he had been informed of the incident at the palace and the time at which he'd authorised Roman's release.

Roman's fists clenched by his sides. He was no stranger to dealing with self-important asses—he'd made a career of protecting arrogant fools with more money than sense. But it was hard to stay professionally disengaged when one of the asses in question was your best friend. Khal had never treated him as 'lesser'—he knew better. But he had not so much as made a phone call to apologise for his oversight.

His friend knew, more than anyone, what time locked in a room could do to him.

Roman tilted his head up to the sun and closed his eyes. He was not in a locked room right now. He was on his own very expensive yacht, which would be out in open water just as soon as it was refuelled. He exhaled slowly, visualising the clear blue waters of Isla Arista, his own private haven.

Moments passed before his visualisation was interrupted by a loud car horn. He opened one eye and sighed as he saw a sleek black limousine edging its way through the crowds on the main street, flanked by four Monteverrian policemen on Vespas.

The Sheikh of Zayyar did not simply take a taxi, he supposed dryly as he reached forward to drain the last of his coffee and then tilted his head back to the sunshine. When he finally looked up again Khal was standing a foot away, his face a mask of cool fury.

'It was nice of you to finally come to my rescue, *bratik*.' Roman raised a brow from his perch on the deckchair, but made no move to stand and greet his oldest friend.

Khal's mouth twisted. 'I was under the impression that the untouchable Roman Lazarov never *needed* help.'

'And *I* was under the impression that our friendship came before brown-nosing the King of Monteverre.' Roman spoke quietly, venom in every word.

Right now, looking at Khal in his perfectly pressed white royal robes, a good old-fashioned punching match didn't sound like the worst way to start his day. Back on the streets of St Petersburg it was the way most fights were resolved. Fighting had sometimes been the only way not to starve.

Roman scowled, realising the hunger in his gut was doing nothing to help his already agitated mood and the dark memories of his past threatening his control.

'I was not aware that you had been held in custody until this morning.'

Khal interrupted his thoughts, frowning with genuine concern.

Roman tipped his head back, propping one foot lazily up on the low table in front of him. People generally afforded the almighty Sheikh of Zayyar a certain level of ceremony and pomp. But not him. He usually went out of his way to take Khal down a peg whenever they were alone.

'Oh, just five hours in a windowless room with my hands cuffed behind my back—no big deal.'

'I find it hard to sympathise, considering you'd held my future wife hostage like a common criminal,' Khal said simply.

'An interesting choice of words, *Your Highness*,' Roman snarled, derision in every syllable.

A silence fell between them—not the comfortable kind that came from years of close friendship. This was a silence filled with tension and frustration.

A friendship like theirs had no clear rules, different as they were.

Khal came from a long line of royalty—had been educated and privileged and born with power in his blood. Whereas Roman had fought for everything he owned, clawing his way out of the gutter he had been abandoned in as a child. Over the years he had refined his harsh manners and learned how to act like a gentleman, but underneath he would always bear the marks of his past. The darkness had branded him—quite literally—and that was something his friend had no experience of.

Khal cleared his throat loudly. 'You know, in ten years I don't think you've changed one bit.'

Roman ignored the barely veiled insult, shrugging as he put one leg casually across the table. 'I have a lot more money.'

'And an even bigger ego.' Khal frowned.

'Need I remind you that I came here as a favour? I did not *have* to dirty my hands for you, Khal. No matter what debts I may owe you.'

'Is that the only reason you came? And here I was thinking you cared for my happiness.' Khal's mouth tightened. 'Four years is a long time to hold on to your guilt, Lazarov.'

Roman shook his head, standing to pace to the railing that edged the upper deck. He had enough painful memories affecting his concentration today—he didn't need more reminders of the long line of blackness he left in his wake.

'I came here because you needed help, *bratik*. Nothing more.'

For the first time Khal looked weary as he rubbed a hand across his clean-shaven face. He sat down in the deckchair Roman had vacated and stared up at the clear sky above them.

'This whole situation is rapidly getting away from me. My trip was supposed to be simple and straight-forward, tying everything up. And now I stand to lose everything I have staked.'

Roman frowned at his friend's unusual display of weakness. 'It will be fine. I will apologise to the Princess and smooth things over for you.'

Khal looked at him, realisation dawning on his dark features. 'You don't know? The Princess has disappeared, Roman. Half the Palace Guard is out searching for her.'

Roman froze with surprise. 'Disappeared? I just spoke with her last night.'

'You *spoke* with her?' Khal's voice raised an octave. 'What on earth would possess you to speak with her after what you'd put her through?'

'She had me put through far worse, trust me.'

'So this is even more your fault than I had originally thought?'

'Khal, I had the tunnel blocked, extra guards assigned. How on earth could she have just walked out of there?'

Khal shook his head. 'Clearly she wanted to get away badly enough to risk her own safety. What did you say to her?'

'We barely spoke two words. Mainly she insulted me and then she walked away.'

Both men were silent for a long moment, facing off in the midday heat.

'The girl is reckless,' Roman said darkly. 'Are you sure that you want to marry someone so... unpredictable?'

'My kingdom needs it. So it will be done.' Khal smoothed down the front of his robes. 'I have been heavy-handed with my approach so far. I worry that perhaps I have scared her off completely.'

'How so?'

'I ordered a stricter security regime. I needed to make sure she was protected adequately before her name was linked with mine. In case...'

Roman saw the haunted look in his friend's eyes and immediately stopped. How had he not realised before now?

He moved towards him, placing a hand heavily on his shoulder. 'Khal... I understand why you felt the need to ensure her security…believe me. But there *is* such a thing as smothering with safety.'

'We both know the risks for any woman who is by my side,' Khal said, standing to his feet.

The moment of weakness had passed and he was once again the formidable and controlled Sheikh of Zayyar. But Roman could still sense the heaviness in the air, the unspoken worries that he knew plagued his friend and had likely tortured him for the past four years.

Nothing would bring back his friend's wife. Her sudden death had shifted something in the easy friendship that had once bonded them together, and nothing would erase the pain of knowing that he hadn't been there in Khal's time of need.

Roman cleared his throat. 'I will go and find the Princess,' he said gruffly.

'No. Definitely not.' Khal turned back to him, crossing his arms. 'Your presence would only aggravate the situation further.'

'If it was my actions that caused her to rethink the engagement, then let me be the one to apologise and bring her back.' Roman pushed his hands into the pockets of his trousers, feeling the weight of his own error settle somewhere in his gut. 'This is *my* fault.'

'Yes. It is.' Khal raised one brow. 'And I hate not knowing if I can trust you to fix it.'

Roman's jaw clenched. Khal was like a brother to

him—his *bratik*. The closest thing to a family member he had ever chosen for himself.

'You have trusted me with your life in the past. Are you telling me you don't think I'm capable of retrieving one errant little princess?'

'This is important to me, Roman.'

'I will bring her back. You have my word,' Roman said, meaning every syllable.

He would find the little siren and bring her back to her royal duty if it was the last thing he did.

This had been a terrible plan.

Olivia slumped down in her seat, tucking an errant strand of bright red hair back into her dark, wide floppy-brimmed hat. Because of the dark sunglasses she wore, and the rather plain white shift dress, thankfully so far nobody had looked at her twice.

Olivia sighed. Had she really been so naïve as to think that she could just check in to the next commercial flight without question? The realisation of what she had almost done suddenly paralysed her with fear. She had almost broken the law, for goodness' sake.

She was hyper aware of her surroundings, noticing every little movement of the people in the departures hall. Every time one of the airport security guards looked at her she unconsciously held her breath, waiting for the moment when they would realise who she was and unceremoniously haul her back to the palace. And to her father.

She didn't even know exactly what she was trying to achieve here. Honestly, had she really been so immature as to think that her father would take her more seriously just because she had attempted to run away from her engagement? In reality this little stunt had done nothing but ensure that she would have even less freedom than before.

She closed her eyes, leaning her head back against the seat and wishing that she had never come up with this stupid plan. She felt the air shift to her right, a gentle breeze bringing with it an eerily familiar scent of sandalwood and pine.

'A risky choice, hiding in plain sight,' a deeply accented male voice drawled from beside her, bringing memories of strong, muscular arms and eyes like gunmetal.

Roman Lazarov lowered himself casually into the seat beside her and lazily propped one ankle on the opposite knee.

'You really didn't think this through.'

From this angle, all she could see were powerful thighs encased in designer trousers and a pair of expensive leather shoes. She exhaled slowly, realising from the sound of his voice that he must have his face turned towards her. Watching to gauge her reaction.

He was probably congratulating himself on finding her so easily, the brute.

He cleared his throat loudly, waiting for her response.

Olivia pursed her lips and kept her eyes focused straight ahead. She wondered if, perhaps if she waited long enough, he would simply disappear into thin air.

'You have ten seconds to give up your silent act before I announce your presence to this entire airport.' He spoke low, his voice a barely contained growl.

She stiffened. 'You're bluffing.'

'*Look at me.*'

She turned her head at his demand, hardly realising she had obeyed until it was done. His eyes were focused on her, steel-grey and glowing, just as she remembered them. His lips, so full and perfectly moulded, seemed to quirk a little at the sides as his eyes narrowed. It took a moment for her to realise he was silently laughing at her.

'I *was* bluffing.' He smiled in triumph, showing a row of perfectly aligned white teeth.

His smile was aggressively beautiful, just like the rest of him, she thought, with more than a little frustration. She noticed the rather delicious hint of dark stubble that lined his jaw. It somehow made him appear rugged and unrefined, even in his finely tailored clothing. She felt her throat go dry and silently cursed herself.

'If you're wondering how I found you, I simply

followed the enormous trail of breadcrumbs you left in your wake, Printsessa.'

'Don't call me that here,' Olivia murmured. The hum of noise in the airport was loud enough, but she didn't want to draw any more attention than was needed.

He raised one brow, but nodded.

Olivia took a sharp breath, a slight tremor audible in her throat. 'If I asked you to go, and pretend you'd never found me...'

'That will never happen.' He half smiled as he spoke the words, a small indentation appearing just left of his lips.

The man had dimples, she thought wildly. That was hardly fair, was it?

Before she could react, he had reached down and grabbed the small document she had been holding tightly in her hands. As she watched, he opened it, tilting his head to one side as he read.

After a long moment he looked up, meeting her eyes with disbelief. 'You planned to use this?'

'Initially, yes. But then I thought better of it.'

'A wise choice, considering identity fraud is a very serious crime. Even for princesses.'

Olivia remained silent, staring down at the red mark on her fingers from where she had clutched the maid's passport so hard it had almost cut off her circulation.

It had been a careless plan from the start, one

borne of desperation and anger. If she had got caught... The thought tightened her throat. Fraud simply wasn't something that was in her nature, luckily. Meaning that she had come no closer than eight feet from the check-in desk before she had turned on her heel and run. Leaving her sitting on this damned chair for the past two hours, frantically wondering where to go next.

Olivia shook off the ridiculous self-pity and forced herself to get a handle on her emotions. She was emotionally and physically exhausted. Any sleep she had got last night had been plagued by dreams of being trapped in tunnels with no way out, and a man's voice calling to her from the darkness. When she had finally got up this morning it had been with the grim intent of getting as far away from Monteverre as possible, and yet here she was, less than an hour's distance from the palace and already captured.

The entire plan had been stupid and impulsive from the start. Honestly, where had she really thought she would go once she'd walked out of the palace gates? She didn't even have the right to hold her own passport, for goodness' sake. Everything in her life was planned and controlled by others. She didn't even have enough freedom to run away properly.

Roman was still looking at her intently. She could feel the heat of his gaze on the side of her face, almost as though he burned her simply by being near. He made her feel as though she were on show and he was the only person in the audience. The intensity of his presence was something she simultaneously wanted to bask in and run far away from.

'I'm not running from my title.' She spoke solemnly, knowing he could never understand.

'Then what are you running from?' His voice was low and serious, and his gaze still pinned on hers with silvery intensity.

Olivia took a deep breath, knowing this conversation had to end. He was not on her side, no matter how sympathetic he pretended to be.

'It's not safe for you to be wandering alone.' His voice took on a steely edge. 'I feel responsible for your decision to leave the palace. Perhaps you felt that yesterday reflected badly on your future husband—'

Again the 'future husband' talk. Olivia stood up, feeling her blood pressure rise with sheer frustration.

Roman's hand took hold of hers, pulling her back down to a sitting position. His voice was low, somewhere near her right ear, as he spoke in chilling warning, 'Don't make any more impulsive moves, Printsessa. I might seem gentle, but I can assure you if you run from me again I might not be quite so civilised in hauling you back where you belong.'

Her heart hammered hard in her chest, and the skin along her neck and shoulders tingled and prickled with the effects of his barely veiled threat.

'My car is parked at the door. We can do this the easy way or the hard way.'

Olivia briefly considered her options—or lack thereof. Was she really prepared to risk what might happen if she resisted? The memory of his powerful arms encircling her in her dressing room sprang to her mind. For a moment she sat completely still, wondering if the frisson of electricity that coursed through her veins was one of trepidation or one of something infinitely more dangerous.

She stood, spine straight, and began walking towards the entrance. He followed, as she'd expected, his muscular frame falling into step by her side. His hand cupped her elbow, steering her out into the daylight towards a gleaming white luxury model car with privacy-tinted windows. Not the kind of car she would have expected from a new money playboy with a taste for danger.

Her silent captor slid into the driver's seat across from her, his warm, masculine scent filling the small space. He didn't look at her as he manoeuvred the car out of the airport and through the maze of roads that led to the motorway.

She covertly glanced at him from behind the safety of her sunglasses. Strong, masculine hands handled the wheel with expert ease. She noticed the top two buttons of his black shirt lay open and his sleeves had been rolled up along forearms that practically bulged with muscle. Strange black markings encircled his skin just above his shirt cuff—tribal, perhaps, but she couldn't see more than the edge.

Of *course* he had a tattoo, she thought, biting her lip as she wondered just how many he might have. And where they might be…

'You are staring. Something you'd like to say?'

His low, accented voice jolted her and she averted her eyes, looking straight ahead, curling her fingers together in her lap. 'I was simply wondering if you will be delivering me to my father or to the Sheikh.'

'So dramatic.' He sighed. 'You make it sound like you are a shipment of goods.'

'I might as well be,' she muttered under her breath. 'It's hard not to feel like a piece of livestock. Being traded from one barbarian to another.'

His hands seemed to tighten on the wheel. 'I'd prefer if you didn't use your pity party to insult my friend in that fashion. "Barbarian" is not a term he would take lightly.'

'Mr Lazarov, at this point I can't say that I particularly care.'

'I suggest that you start caring,' Roman gritted, moving the car off the motorway and towards the mountain range that separated them from the Grand Palace.

Twenty minutes in this pampered princess's company and he was tempted to stop the car and make her walk the rest of the way.

She was a puzzle, this fiery redhead. A spoilt, impulsive, dangerous puzzle, all wrapped up in one very tempting package. He would not feel guilty for being attracted to Khal's fiancée. A man would have to be blind not to see the raw sensual appeal in Olivia Sandoval. But, unlike her, he had his impulses under control. It was not hard to brush off attraction when he could tell that all that lay beneath her flawless skin and designer curves was a spoilt, bored little royal on the hunt for a thrill.

'Your father has asked that you be returned to the palace as soon as possible,' Roman said, noticing how her body seemed to tense at the mention of the King. 'But I feel that you and your fiancé need to speak first.'

'He is *not* my fiancé,' Olivia gritted.

'Oh, so that's what is going on here. You decided to break the engagement by running away. How very mature.'

Roman felt his jaw tighten with anger for his friend, for the future of two nations that was hanging in the balance all because of one woman.

'No, *I* haven't decided anything. That's the point!'

Roman heard the slight tremor in her voice and turned briefly to see she had her head in her hands. 'Look, if this is bridal jitters, I'm sure there's plenty of time before the wedding—'

Her head snapped up and she pinned him with the most ferocious icy blue-green gaze. 'Do you honestly think I would risk my reputation, my safety, over a little case of *bridal jitters*?'

'I only met you yesterday.' He shrugged.

It was true—he didn't know very much about her except that she had a deep-rooted mistrust of men and a mean left hook.

'This isn't something to speak about with a stranger.'

'At least you're listening…somewhat.' She sighed. 'Even if you think the worst of me.'

He said nothing, concentrating on the road as they edged around the mountain face. He could have taken the new, modern tunnel that bisected the mountain entirely. But this was a new country for him and he enjoyed the scenic routes.

Olivia lay her head back on the seat, her voice low and utterly miserable. 'How can a woman suddenly have a fiancé when she hasn't heard or even decided to accept a marriage proposal?'

'You mean…Khal didn't formally propose? This is what's upset you?'

'No. He did *not* formally propose,' she said, mocking laughter in her voice. 'I only met the Sheikh yesterday for the first time—at the races. Five minutes after my father informed me that I would be marrying him.'

CHAPTER FOUR

ROMAN FELT HIS brain stumble over her words. 'That is impossible.'

'Welcome to my life.' A deep sigh left her chest. 'Apparently Monteverre has reverted to the Middle Ages.'

'The Sheikh assured me that all the arrangements have been made. That he is simply here to make the formal announcement of your intended marriage.'

'The only arrangement that has been made is a business one. Evidently the bride was not important enough to be let in on the plans.'

She laughed once—a low, hollow sound that made Roman's gut clench.

'I'm twenty-six years old and suddenly I'm expected to tie myself to a stranger for the rest of my life.'

A tense silence fell between them and Roman took a moment to process this new information. Khal had not been honest with him. And if there was one thing that Roman Lazarov despised it was being taken for a fool. Khal had said the Princess was his future bride, leaving him with the assumption that the woman had consented to the marriage. Now, knowing that she hadn't...

Call him old-fashioned, but he believed a woman had a right to her own freedom, her own mind. Growing up on the streets, he had seen first-hand just what happened when men decided simply to assume a woman's consent.

The Princess had called Khal a barbarian, but Roman knew that was the furthest thing from the truth. He wanted to believe that this was all a misunderstanding—that Khal had been misled by the King into believing his intended bride was a willing participant in all this. However...he knew the single-minded ruthlessness that possessed the Sheikh whenever his nation's future lay in the balance.

He had said himself that this marriage was vital to Zayyar's future. Perhaps it was vital enough to overlook a reluctant bride?

They rounded a particularly sharp bend and the road began to descend towards the lush green valley that spread out below. This country had its own particular charm—there was no denying it, he thought as he took in the glittering sea in the distance.

A small lay-by had been built into the outer curve of the road—a safe place for people to stop and take photographs while stretching their legs. Making a snap decision, Roman slowed down, manoeuvring the car into a vacant spot in the deserted lay-by and bringing them to a stop.

'What are you doing?' Olivia's brows furrowed.

'I need a moment,' he said, taking the keys with him as he stood away from the car, just in case his passenger had any ideas. The lay-by was deserted, and the road far too steep for her to get anywhere on foot.

He braced his hands on the glittering granite wall and took a moment to inhale the fresh mountain air deeply. There was something about the sight of completely unspoiled nature that deeply affected him. He had spent far too much of his youth surrounded by concrete buildings and garbage-scented air.

The sea beckoned to him in the distance. His yacht was ready to leave the moment he returned— ready to sail out into the open sea, where he would be free of this troubled royal family and their tangled web.

All he had to do was drop her off at the palace and he was home free.

Why he was hesitating all of a sudden, he did not know, but something was stopping him from completing his directive without questioning it further. He heard the car's passenger door close gently and turned to see the Princess come to a stop at the wall beside him.

'This is my favourite view in all of Monteverre,' she said. There was not a hint of sadness in her voice. It was just fact, stated without emotion.

He realised that since the moment he had held her captive in the tunnel he had not seen her resort to tears once. No one, including him, would have judged her for breaking down in the face of an unknown captor. She had a backbone of steel, and yet she had not been able to follow through with her plan to use the fraudulent passport. She clearly drew the line at breaking the law, and could not blur her own moral guidelines even in apparent desperation.

'What exactly were you hoping to achieve by running?' he asked, directing his question to the side of her face as she continued to stare out at the distance.

'I don't know.' She nipped lightly at her bottom lip. 'I just needed the chance to come to a decision myself. Some time to weigh up my options. I have no idea what life is like away from my guards and my responsibilities, and yet here I am, expected to blindly trade one set of palace walls for another.'

He couldn't disagree with her logic.

'When I agreed to perform the security operation yesterday, I presumed that your marriage had already been arranged.' He ran a hand across his jaw, the memory of his handling of her raw and uncomfortable. 'Had I known the situation was not what it seemed I would not have agreed to it.'

She shrugged, defeat evident in the downward slope of her slim shoulders.

'I will take you to Khal. You can address your

concerns to him directly. That is generally how adults resolve such situations.'

Olivia stared at him with disbelief. 'I am not a child. Despite being treated like one time and time again.' She braced her two hands on the wall, her perfectly manicured nails in stark contrast against the stone. 'I have no interest in pleading my case to a man I do not know. Besides, do you think I would have done this if I wasn't already completely sure that my voice will hold no weight in this situation?'

Roman pinched the bridge of his nose, a low growl forming in his chest. 'Damn it, I do not have time for this. I could have been halfway across the Mediterranean by now.'

She turned to him, one hand on her hip. 'I'm sorry that our political situation is such an inconvenience to your playboy lifestyle, Mr Lazarov.'

She took a step away, her shoulders squared with frustration, before she turned back to face him.

'You know what? I'm tired of this too. You may as well just take me to the Sheikh right now, so that I can reject his proposal in person. If his choice in friends is anything to go by, I'm sure I won't be missing out on too much.'

'You presume I *care* how you pampered royals resolve your issues?'

'You wouldn't be here if you didn't.'

'The only reason I am here is because you chose to be a coward rather than face the situation head-on.'

Hurt flashed in her eyes and he suddenly felt like the world's biggest heel.

'I don't know what to do,' she said honestly, her eyes meeting his with sudden vulnerability. 'I know that marrying the Sheikh is the right choice for my people. Despite what you might think, I *do* care about this kingdom—very much. If I didn't, I would have already said no.'

The silence that fell between them was thick and tension-filled, although the air was cooling down now, as the sun dropped lower in the sky and evening fell across the mountain.

She had accused him of tightening her cage yesterday, and today it couldn't be more true. The idea of pretending he hadn't found her in the first place was tempting…but no matter how much it would simplify his life he knew that a woman like her wasn't safe alone in the world. He knew more than anyone that there were far too many opportunistic criminals out there, just waiting for a chance at a high-class victim. Keeping rich people safe was his business, after all.

'I have never been out in public away from the Palace Guard for this length of time. It's nice…not being surrounded by an entourage.'

'You want a taste of freedom,' he said plainly, and the sudden realisation was like clouds parting to reveal blue sky after a storm.

'Isn't that what all runaways want?' She smiled

sadly. 'But we both know how that has worked out for me so far.'

'I can't just let you walk away from me, Princess. You know that.'

He pondered the situation, despising his own need to problem-solve. Khal needed this marriage to go ahead. That was his directive here. There was no point returning the Princess only for her to reject the marriage completely. But maybe he could offer a solution that would benefit everyone involved.

Everyone except him, that was.

He frowned, hardly believing he was even entertaining the idea, but words escaped his mouth and he knew he had to trust his instinct. 'What if I could offer you a temporary freedom of sorts?' he asked slowly, watching as her face tipped up and her eyes regarded him with suspicion.

'I would ask what exactly you mean by "temporary".'

'I can offer you some time alone in which you can come to a decision about your marriage.'

'Or lack thereof?'

'Exactly.'

'How would you do that?' she asked. 'And, more importantly, *why* would you?'

'Don't worry about how—just trust that I am a man of my word. If I say you will be undisturbed then I mean it. But you would have your side of the bargain to hold up.'

'I'm listening.'

'All I ask is that you take time to consider all aspects of the union. I believe that you would be making a mistake in walking away from this engagement. Khal is a great man,' he said truthfully.

He was careful not to mention the small fact that she was a flight risk who would likely end up in real trouble if the situation wasn't contained. This was containment at its most extreme. He had somehow gone from holding a princess hostage to volunteering to take one on as his guest.

He waited while she visibly weighed up her options before him, worrying at her lower lip with her teeth. Her mouth was a dusky pink colour, he noticed. No lipstick or gloss, just pure silky rose flesh. She flashed him a glance and he quickly averted his gaze, looking back out at the view.

In that moment he instantly regretted his offer to salvage his friend's union. He had the sudden uncomfortable thought that perhaps he had just voluntarily offered to step out onto a tightrope with everything hanging in the balance.

But even as he began to regret his offer she nodded her head once, murmuring her acceptance.

And just like that the deal was done.

He had never gone back on a deal in the past, and he wouldn't be starting now. Self-doubt held no place in his life. He trusted his own self-control, his own loyalty to those he cared for. And so he walked her back to the car and dutifully avoided looking down at the swell of her curves as she sashayed in front of him.

'I still don't understand why you are doing this for me.' She looked up at him through long russet lashes, and he saw a smattering of freckles appearing high on her cheeks in the evening sun.

'Consider it a wedding gift,' he gritted, shutting the door with finality and steeling himself for the drive ahead.

Olivia stepped out on the deserted deck of the yacht and watched as they drew nearer and nearer to land. The evening was fast fading to pink as dusk approached. She wondered if maybe she should be worried that she had no idea where Roman was taking her, but really the destination itself didn't matter. So long as it was far enough away from the palace for her to be able to breathe again.

With every mile that had passed since they'd set sail from Puerto Reina harbour she had felt the unbearable tension begin to ease and a sense of sharp relief take its place. But her newfound sense of freedom still held an unpleasant tinge of guilt around the edges. As if a dark cloud was hovering somewhere in her peripheral vision, just waiting to spill over and wreak havoc on her fleeting sense of calm.

She was doing the right thing, wasn't she? Taking time away from the royal bubble in a controlled manner was the mature course of action. Despite what others might think, she knew she had a very important decision to make. This wasn't so simple as making the best choice for herself—putting the rest of her life first and repercussions be damned. She had been raised always to hold Monteverre in greater esteem than herself. To value the people more than she did her own family. But what happened when her own family didn't seem to value her happiness at all?

Her eyes drifted across the deck to where her slim black handbag sat atop a sun lounger. Inside that bag she held all the information she had found about the foundation that her grandmother had left in her name. Information on all of the amazing work that it had carried out since her passing ten years ago.

She wasn't quite ready to share what she had uncovered with anyone just yet.

At the moment, the bottom line was clear. Her father had said that she had no alternative but to marry the Sheikh and she had agreed with him, Going against a union arranged by the King now would have very real, very severe ramifications. Either way, her life was about to change drastically.

It was no big deal, really, she thought with a slightly panicked intake of breath. Sign her life away to a loveless marriage in order to save her kingdom or have her title stripped away for ever. No big deal at all.

She closed her eyes, breathing in the cool sea air

and willing her mind to slow down. She had spent two days going around and around in circles already, and the effect made her temples feel fit to burst. Was it any wonder she had made such a rash decision to run away from it all?

She exhaled slowly, opening her eyes to find that the yacht was now sailing alongside the coast of the seemingly deserted island they had been approaching. The place looked completely wild—like something from a movie. But as they rounded an outcrop of rocks she was suddenly looking at a crescent-shaped coastline formed out of ragged black rocks and golden sand. A tall white lighthouse stood on the far coast in the distance, atop a lush green cliff. And a small marina was situated at the furthest end of the bay, in the shade of the cliffs.

She gradually felt the yacht lose speed until it began the process of mooring at the end of the long white floating dock.

Roman was still nowhere to be seen, she thought as she scanned what she could see of the upper decks. The yacht was huge, and he had disappeared almost immediately after depositing her in one of the lower deck living rooms.

She was still not quite sure why he had decided to give her this time in the first place. She doubted he felt pity for her, considering his disdain for 'pampered royals', as he had so delicately labelled her. But he had seemed genuinely surprised to hear that the marriage situation was not all that it seemed.

She was not naïve enough to believe that he was on her side, but she hoped that he understood her motivations a little more at least.

Still, she would do well to remember where his loyalties lay. He was determined to see her accept Sheikh Khal's proposal—there was no doubt in her mind about that. She imagined that Roman Lazarov was not the type of man to give up on something without putting up a good fight first.

Surprisingly, the thought of debating her future with him didn't fill her with the same dread that she had felt in her father's presence the day before. She couldn't quite explain it... He spoke to her like a person, not as someone lesser. Or, worse, as a princess. He wasn't afraid to look into her eyes as he spoke, unlike most others who met her.

He had listened to her today. She would never let him know how much that had meant to her. He was not a friend—she knew that. But maybe he didn't have to be her enemy.

As though conjured by her thoughts, Roman suddenly emerged from a door to her right, speaking to someone on the phone in a deep, throaty language she presumed to be his native Russian. He had made no move to interact with her in the hours since they had set sail from Monteverre.

He looked tired, she noticed, and yet his dark shirt

and trousers barely held a single crease. She, on the other hand, was rumpled and in dire need of a shower and a full night of sleep. She smoothed the front of her dress self-consciously and turned herself to face him, shoulders held high.

He ended the call with one click and took a moment to tilt his face up to the view of the vibrant overgrown landscape around them. For a moment the harsh lines around his mouth relaxed and his eyes seemed to glow silver in the evening light. She realised with surprise that the look on his face was something very close to contentment. She'd not yet seen him with anything but hostility in his features, and she had to admit the man had very inviting lips when he wasn't smirking or insulting her.

'We still have a short drive from here,' he said, taking a quick look at his watch and motioning for the single cabin porter to take care of their luggage. 'I hope you don't get motion sickness.'

Before she could question that statement, he gestured for her to follow him down the steps onto the whitewashed boards of the marina. She practically had to run to catch up with him.

'Where are we?' she asked, her short legs struggling to keep up with his long strides.

'My very own island paradise,' he said simply, not bothering to slow down until they'd reached a dirt road at the end of the dock. Roman stopped beside a small, open-sided white Jeep and turned to face her, one hand braced lazily on the mud-spattered door frame as he held it open for her.

'Jump in, Princess.' His lips quirked.

That was a challenge if ever she'd heard one. He likely expected her to throw a fit of pique, demanding transportation that better befitted her station.

She smiled sweetly, holding up her white skirt to protect it from the worst of the dirt, and hoisted herself up into the cab without complaint. Within minutes the engine was roaring loudly and a cloud of dust flew around them as they began a steady climb up the cliffs.

'When you said you could guarantee privacy, I didn't realise you meant to maroon me on a desert island.' She forced an easy tone, trying to hide the breathlessness from her voice.

He didn't immediately respond, so she filled the silence by commenting on the views of the coast below as they drove higher and higher, weaving in and out of the treeline. As they bounced over a particularly rough stretch of terrain her shoulder was jammed hard against the window and she let out a little squeak of alarm.

She turned to see that he was smirking once more. She fought the sudden, irrational urge to punch him in the bicep.

'Judging by the transportation, am I to expect a

rustic mud hut for my stay?' She gripped her seatbelt with all her might, her resolve slipping fast.

'I'm not here to act as your tour guide.' He shrugged, uninterested, his jaw tightening as he shifted gears and the terrain seemed to level out. 'I'll be sure to have your tent inspected for cockroaches, at least.'

She had never actually slept in a tent. It would be a drastic change from her usual surroundings, but she rather thought she might enjoy the novelty.

Just as she turned to say this to him she caught sight of something sparkling in the distance. The land began to slope downwards towards the lower terrain again, revealing a spectacular side view of a very large, very sleek, modern villa.

As they descended a short driveway Olivia felt her breath catch at the view that spread out before them. She could see the entire island from this vantage point. The evening sky was tinged pink and orange as the sun sank lower and lower towards the jade-green sea.

'Wow...' she breathed, her awestruck brain not quite able to form anything more eloquent after the stunning visual onslaught.

A small white-haired man appeared at the door as they stepped out of the car. He looked immediately to Roman with raised brows.

'You did not mention a guest, sir,' he said, his smile forced and pointed.

'Jorge, how many times do I have to tell you not to call me sir just because we are in company?' Roman grunted.

'It's more professional.' Jorge shrugged, trying and failing to keep his voice low.

'You are *far* from professional.' Roman smirked, clapping the other man on the shoulder with friendly familiarity. 'Ridiculously capable and efficient? Of course. But not professional in the least. That's why I hired you.'

The two men looked back to see Olivia watching the odd exchange with interest.

'Olivia, this is my right-hand man, Jorge. He travels with me to my homes as housekeeper and chef.'

Roman seemed suddenly preoccupied as he took out his phone and clicked a few buttons.

'Show her around and set her up in the white guest room.'

Olivia frowned as he began to walk away without another word. 'You mean you won't be giving me the grand tour yourself?' she called, half joking but actually quite shocked at his blatant disregard.

A harsh laugh escaped his lips as he continued to power across the hallway, away from her. 'I am not in the hospitality business. I thought you would have noticed that by now.'

And with that he disappeared through a doorway at the end of the hall, leaving her alone with his very apologetic housekeeper.

* * *

Roman ended the call with a double-click and laid his phone down hard on the marble patio table. In almost ten years of friendship he had never heard his friend curse.

Khal had been stunned at the revelation that the Princess was being strong-armed into their union by her father. But, ever practical, he had asked if there was a chance she might go ahead with it. Roman had answered truthfully—saying that he believed the Princess was just seeking a break from the heightened security measures.

'Give her time,' he had said. 'I will ensure she returns to accept your proposal.'

Khal trusted him to guard his future bride. There wasn't another person on this earth that Roman would be doing this for. He was not a personal bodyguard. He specialised in hard security. Elite risk assessments, intruder prevention, high-tech electronic systems and such. He did not have the refined people skills that were needed to work one-on-one in this kind of setting.

And yet here he was, babysitting a runaway princess on the island that he made a point to keep free of unwelcome guests.

If he had ever been a drinker now would be an excellent time for copious amounts of alcohol in which to drown his dark mood. He leaned heavily against the glass rail that lined the balcony of his master suite, looking out at the horizon where the sun had begun to dip into the Mediterranean Sea.

A sudden splash from below caught his attention and he looked down to see a creamy silhouette cutting easily across the bottom of the pool.

She had started her holiday straight away, it seemed, he thought darkly as his fist tightened on the rail.

Her head and bare shoulders broke the surface of the water as she reached the infinity ledge. Her red hair was dark and heavy on her shoulders; she hadn't bothered to tie it up. She leaned against the side of the pool, pale shoulders glistening with moisture above a bright red one-piece bathing suit. He could see the outline of long, slim legs under the water.

Roman felt the darkness inside him roar to life.

He wanted her.

He growled to himself, turning away from the tantalising view with a jaw that suddenly felt like iron. He stalked across his suite into the large white and chrome bathroom. The large floor-to-ceiling mirror showed his frustration in high definition. His pupils were dark, his nostrils flared with anger as he began unbuttoning his shirt.

It had been a while since he had been with anyone—that was all this was. His body was reacting to its recent deprivation in the most primal way possible.

He had never been good at denying himself something he wanted with this kind of intensity.

A more emotionally charged person might say it had something to do with a childhood full of being denied, he thought darkly. *He* knew better. It was simply a part of him—a part of how he was put together. It was what drove him to the heights of success, always wanting more.

All he knew was that his wealth had brought along with it the delicious ability to gratify his every whim instantly. Whether it was a new car or a beautiful woman, he always got what he wanted with minimal effort.

But not her.

She was not his to think about, to look at, to covet.

He was long past his days as a thief, he thought dryly as he divested himself of the rest of his clothing and stepped under the white-hot spray of the shower, feeling the heat seep into his taut shoulder muscles and down his back.

Another man might have opted for a cold spray, but he had spent too much of his life in the cold. He had the best hot shower that money could buy and damn it, he would use it. Even if it only spurred on the heat inside him.

He was unsure whether he was angry with his friend for trusting him so blindly or angry that he did not fully trust himself. He was a sophisticated man, well capable of resisting flimsy attractions. And yet he felt a need to keep some distance between himself and the fiery-haired Olivia, with her sharp wit and unpredictable nature.

He had built his fortune on trusting his own instincts, and everything about Olivia Sandoval signalled danger.

CHAPTER FIVE

As was usual when he stayed on Isla Arista, Roman had instructed Jorge to prepare an evening meal to be served on the terrace. The scent of aromatic rosemary chicken filled his nostrils as he stepped outside and his stomach growled in anticipation.

Olivia already sat at the table, waiting for him. He was surprised to see she had not changed after her swim; instead she was wrapped in an oversized white terrycloth robe from the pool cabana. One bare foot peeked out from where it was tucked under her. His stomach tightened at the sight of a single red-painted toenail.

'I see you are taking your holiday quite literally,' he said, taking the seat opposite her at the long marble table.

She looked down at his crisp white shirt and uncertainty flickered across her features, followed closely by embarrassment. 'Your housekeeper said it was just a quick meal. I wasn't aware that we would eat together,' she said, standing to her feet.

'Sit down,' he said and sighed.

But she vehemently shook her head, promising to be just a few minutes as she hurried away through the terrace doors at lightning speed. He fought the urge to laugh. How ironic that out of both of them it was the member of royalty who felt unfit for polite company.

True to her word, she returned less than ten minutes later. He was relieved to see that she hadn't opted for another dress, and amused that once again she wore white. The simple white linen trousers hugged her curves just as sinfully as the dress had, but thankfully she had chosen a rather sober white button-down blouse that covered her up almost to her chin.

Still, her slim shoulders were completely bare, showing off her perfect alabaster skin. He consciously lowered his gaze, to focus on filling their water glasses.

He made no move to speak. He was tired and hungry and in no mood to make her feel at ease. In fact it was better that she wasn't completely comfortable. That would make two of them.

Ever the efficient host, Jorge soon had the table filled with delicious freshly cooked dishes. Roman loaded his plate with tender chicken, garlic-roasted baby potatoes and seasonal grilled vegetables. No matter where they were in the world—New York, Moscow or this tiny remote island—his housekeeper always managed to find the freshest ingredients. He really should give him another raise...

Roman ate as he always did—until he was completely satisfied. Which usually meant two servings, at least, and then washing his meal down with a single glass of wine from his favourite regional *cantina*.

'Where on earth do you put all that food?'

Roman looked up to see Olivia watching him with open fascination, her fork still toying with the same handful of potatoes she had spooned onto her plate ten minutes previously.

'In my stomach,' he said, keeping his tone neutral. 'You had better follow suit or risk offending the chef.'

'We are not *all* graced with fast metabolisms.' She smiled tightly, putting down her fork and dabbing the corners of her mouth delicately.

'I exercise hard so that I can eat well. Good food is there to be enjoyed.' He fought annoyance as she sat back, clearly done with her food.

'The meal was wonderful—thank you.'

'If you say so, Printsessa,' he said, with just a hint of irony, considering she had barely eaten more than a child's portion. At least she didn't seem to be downing the wine to compensate for her self-imposed starvation.

'Why do you call me that?' she asked. 'I presume it's Russian? Printsessa?'

'My apologies. Do you harbour a preference for the term your subjects use? Your Highness, perhaps?'

She frowned. 'Do you enjoy mocking people for no reason?'

'I enjoy nothing of this situation, Olivia.' He exaggerated the syllables of her name with deliberate slowness and watched with satisfaction as she visibly swallowed.

'I don't understand,' she said, sitting forward, a frown forming between perfectly shaped russet brows. '*You* are the one who offered to bring me here, remember? Nobody forced you to do that. We are practically strangers, and yet you have been nothing but rude and downright hostile since the moment we met.'

'I offered to bring you here so that you would stop running away like a teenager,' he gritted. 'This is not a holiday. And I am not here to entertain a pampered royal seeking one last thrill ride before marriage.'

Her blue-green eyes narrowed with some of the fire he remembered from her dressing room the day before. 'You have made a lot of assumptions about my character in the past twenty-four hours.'

'Like it or not, right now you are in *my* charge. If I am making assumptions, it's because I can.'

'You think you know who I am? Please—enlighten me.' She sat back, crossing one slim leg over the other.

Roman watched the movement, his pulse quickening slightly as his eyes followed the curve of her thigh down to the slim silver-heeled sandals on her feet. 'I do not pretend to know who you are—nothing quite so philosophical.'

He leaned back in his chair, stretching one arm behind his neck. She followed the movement, eyelashes lowered.

'I know your type well enough,' Roman said darkly, and his mind surprised him by conjuring up an image of a familiar face. A pair of blue eyes that had haunted him for almost two decades.

His night of imprisonment must have affected him worse than he thought. The cold sweat from being handcuffed still seemed to coat his skin like dirt, even after the hot shower and plentiful meal.

Thoughts of his past were not a common occurrence these days. Thoughts of Sofiya even less common.

He cleared his throat, irritated at himself and his momentary lapse in keeping his own demons at bay. 'You are young, beautiful and privileged, frustrated with the strict rules designed to protect you. So you go out in search of adventure. A little danger to shake up the monotony.'

'So I'm just another spoilt brat looking for a bit of fun? Is that it?'

Roman shrugged noncommittally, draining the last of his wine. 'You are telling me this *isn't* about rebellion?' he asked, knowing he had hit a nerve when her eyes darted away from his to look out at the inky darkness of the sea in the distance.

'You know, insulting me and my motivation is

hardly going to send me running back to accept your friend's proposal.'

'The only reason you feel insulted is because you are likely used to always hearing what you want to hear.'

Olivia sighed, leaning her head back for a moment and pinching the bridge of her nose. 'I am simply taking a brief reprieve before making one of the most important decisions of my life. No big deal, really.'

'I hate to tell you, but that's just a fancy way of saying you're running away.' He couldn't help but smirk.

'So you have me all figured out, then?' She crossed her arms over her chest, meeting his eyes head-on. 'It must be nice, being so untouchable and faultless.'

Roman shrugged. 'It is not my fault that you dislike being told the truth.'

'What I *dislike*, Mr Lazarov, is that you find it so easy to shove all my class into one pile, simply because we were born with money.' She exhaled heavily. 'In my opinion, that says far more about you than it does me.'

'Is that so?'

'Yes, *it is*. I may have been born into wealth, but that does not automatically take away the fact that I am human.' She stood up, pacing to the stone ledge of the terrace before turning back to him. 'You know nothing of my life—just as I know nothing of yours.'

Roman watched as she looked out at the distant

black waves for a moment, with that same faraway look in her eyes that he had seen the night before. He almost felt guilty for goading her.

He cleared his throat loudly. 'We are getting off-track here. This is about repairing your trust in Sheikh Khal.' He sat a little straighter and laid one leg over his knee. 'Not that it will pose much difficulty. Khal is a good man.'

'I appreciate the vote of confidence,' she said, her voice rasping slightly. 'But I believe the point of this time away is for me to come to a decision alone.'

'No one knows him better than I do. Allow me to put your mind at ease.'

'You are not my friend. And I would do well to remember that. I am taking advantage of some time to clear my head—nothing more. I won't speak of this marriage business with you again.'

Roman raised a brow in question, getting to his feet and walking to stand beside her. '"Business…" An interesting word choice.'

She shrugged one slim shoulder, still looking away from him. 'It's the reality.'

'It is a very complex arrangement, from what I know—it's not just about *you*.'

It was as though he were reading straight from a script her father had written. The sudden reminder of her dilemma settled painfully like a dead weight in between Olivia's shoulders. She was so tense she could scream. She had barely slept in the past twenty-four hours, and that coupled with being in this man's presence made every nerve in her body feel completely on edge.

She felt her throat tighten. 'I may be more sheltered than your average twenty-six-year-old woman, but I know what kind of situation I am in.' She cleared her throat, steeling herself. She would *not* show weakness. 'It's *never* been about me—that's the point.'

'Are you telling me you feel you truly have no choice in the matter?' he asked, a sudden seriousness entering his eyes. 'Because a woman being forced into marriage is something I know Khal would never condone. Nor would I.'

Olivia looked up, taking in his broad stance and the furrow between his brows. Logically, she knew that his concern was for his friend, and not for the inconvenient charge he had been landed with. But for a moment she imagined what it might be like to have that kind of protectiveness completely to herself. She imagined that when a man like Roman cared for a woman he would do it fiercely—no prisoners taken. It seemed that he brought intensity into all aspects of his life.

She shook off the fanciful thoughts, suddenly hyper aware of his broad presence looming mere feet away from her. The warm headiness of his cologne teased her nostrils on the night air. His was the kind of scent that made a girl want to stand closer, to breathe it in. It was dangerous, that smell. It made her want to do dangerous things.

'Your silence doesn't exactly give me any insight.' He leaned back on the stone ledge so that he faced her, his grey eyes strangely dark and unreadable in the warm light of the outdoor lamps.

Olivia sighed, shrugging one shoulder with practised indifference. How could she tell him that the only alternative she had to this marriage was to walk away and lose everything she had grown up to value?

'I am not going to be handcuffed and frogmarched up the aisle, if that's what you mean.'

He raised a brow. 'But there would be consequences if you refused?'

She nodded once, unable to stand still in the face of his intense gaze and unwilling to discuss those consequences with a man who'd made it clear he was firmly on the opposite side. She might have escaped her father's imperious presence, but it seemed she had simply swapped one judgemental know-it-all male for another.

She suddenly felt more alone than ever. Her restless feet took her to the end of the terrace, where the stone tiles gave way to soft, spongy grass.

'I can't remember the last time I walked barefoot in the grass,' she said, more to herself than him, and she took a few tentative steps and sighed with appreciation.

One look back showed her that he was still watching her with that same unreadable expression. It was as though he were trying to categorise her, to pin down exactly what he needed to do to fix the very problem of her.

He had said the Sheikh trusted him to problem-solve. That was all she was to him—a problem. It seemed that was all she was to everyone these days, unless she shut her mouth and did what she was told.

'Olivia, come back from there.' Roman's voice boomed from behind her. 'This time of night it's—'

'You know, I think I can make that decision for myself,' she said, cutting him off mid-speech. It was rude, but she was too irritated to care. 'If I want to walk in the grass, I will. I don't need someone to manage every second of my day.'

She took a few more steps across the grass, putting some space between herself and the surprised, strangely amused smirk that had suddenly spread across his face.

'Suit yourself,' he said quietly, looking down at the expensive watch on his wrist. 'But you're going to regret changing out of that bathing suit.'

She frowned at the cryptic statement, turning to face him. Just as she opened her mouth to question that statement the heavens seemed to open above her. Thick droplets of ice-cold rain fell hard and heavy onto her face, making her gasp as the cold spray got heavier and heavier, spreading through her clothing and down her neck and spine.

She was instantly wet through, and her mind took at least ten seconds before telling her to sprint back towards the house. After a few feet the rain suddenly stopped, and she was left looking into Roman's laughing face.

'I would have warned you about the sprinklers,' he said, crossing his arms. 'But I didn't want to manage your day too much.'

She gasped as the cool night air hit her sodden skin. She looked down at her wet clothes and, to her surprise, felt hysterical laughter bubble up her throat.

Roman frowned, also with surprise, 'What? No angry tirade about my appalling lack of consideration?'

'I'm done with being angry today.' She shook her head. 'If I don't laugh right now I might cry. And I make a point of never doing that.'

She leaned to one side, laughing once more as she began to squeeze the water from her hair. A sudden wicked urge grabbed her, and before she could stop herself she pooled the excess liquid in the palm of her hand and threw it in his direction, watching as it landed with a satisfying splash directly in his face.

'I'm sorry,' she said quickly, trying to curb her laughter as she took in his thunderous expression.

He took a step towards her and she felt her breath catch.

'You can't throw the first punch and then retreat with an apology.' His voice was dark and silky on the night air. 'You sell yourself short. That was an excellent aim.'

'I'm not sorry, then.' She smirked, realising with a sudden jolt that she was flirting with him. And that he was flirting back.

The way he was looking at her coupled with the silent darkness of the night surrounding them made her almost imagine that this was a different moment in time entirely. That they weren't just strangers forced into each other's company by circumstance.

She imagined normal people laughed like this and poked fun at one another without fear of making a faux pas. It felt good, being normal.

'You've got quite a wild temper hidden underneath all those royal manners.' He took another step closer.

'I manage to keep it in check most of the time.'

'But not around me.' It was a statement, not a question.

'Don't flatter yourself.' She smiled nervously.

He stood little more than a foot away now, his warm scent clouding around her. She was wet and bedraggled, but she didn't want to leave just yet. She didn't want to end this—whatever it was that was passing between them. After a day filled with confrontation and being on the defensive, it was nice to lose the serious tone—even if for a brief moment.

She crossed her arms under her breasts, feeling the cold air prickle her skin into gooseflesh.

'*Khristos*, why didn't you say you were freezing?'

He reached out to touch her arm, the movement shocking them both as their eyes met in the half-darkness. It was a touch too far. They both knew it. And yet his hand stayed, gripping the soft skin just above her elbow. She shivered again, and this time it was nothing to do with the chill.

She noticed his expression darken suddenly. The air between them filled with a strange sizzling energy and his fingers flexed against her skin just a fraction.

She realised his gaze had moved below her chin. Self-consciously she looked down—and felt the air rush from her lungs in one long drawn-out breath.

Her white blouse.

She might as well be standing in front of him completely naked for all the coverage the wet piece of fabric was offering her. Of *course* tonight had to be the night when, in her haste to dress, she had decided a bra wasn't necessary. And of *course* the cool breeze had resulted in both taut peaks standing proudly to attention.

'Oh, God...'

She took in another breath, silently willing herself to laugh it off, but her mind stumbled clumsily over itself as she took in the obvious heat in his gaze. His eyes were dark and heavy-lidded as they lifted to meet hers. There was no mistaking it now. The silent strum of sensual heat that thrummed in the air between them.

It was a strange feeling—wanting to hide from the intensity of his gaze and bask in it all at the same time. He made her feel warm in places she hadn't known she could feel heat. It was as though her body was silently begging her to move towards him.

What would she do if he suddenly closed the gap between them and laid his lips hungrily on hers? Would he taste as sinfully good as he smelled?

She could suddenly think of nothing else.

What felt like hours passed, when really it was a matter of minutes. All the while his hand remained where it was, scorching her skin. Branding her.

When he finally turned his face away she fought the urge to step closer. To take the moment back. But then she followed his gaze and spied the housekeeper, quietly tidying their dinner dishes away nearby, with all the practised quietness of a professional.

She took one deliberate step away and crossed her arms over her chest, covering herself. His hand fell to his side and the haze of open lust disappeared from his features almost as quickly as it had come.

She wondered how he managed to look both furious and guilt-ridden at the same time. What would have happened if she had given in to that impulse and simply leaned forward to close the gap between them?

As though he'd heard her thoughts, a furrow appeared on his brow. He cleared his throat loudly, turning back to his housekeeper without another glance in her direction. 'Grab a towel for Miss Sandoval before she freezes.'

His cold, uncaring tone only added to the sudden chill that spread through her.

Without saying goodnight, or even looking in her direction, Roman disappeared through the terrace doors, leaving her standing alone, confused and embarrassed in her sodden clothes.

The walls of his master suite were bathed in a cold powder-blue light when Roman awoke. As usual he had not dreamed, but sleep had taken much longer than usual to claim him. And even then it had been fitful and broken at best. It was as though his entire body had thrummed with an intense nervous energy that refused to allow him any real rest.

Never one to remain in bed once his eyes had opened, Roman stood and threw on his jogging shorts.

In less than five minutes he was stretching on the steps that led to the beach. Within another ten he had completed two laps of the mile-long sandy inlet and worked up a healthy sweat. He ran barefoot on the damp sand until his chest heaved and his muscles burned with effort. And then he ran some more.

Usually a good run was enough to rid him of any

thoughts strong enough to affect his sleep. A self-inflicted punishment of sorts, for those times when he knew his mind had begun to grow weak and was in need of strengthening. A weak mind had no place in his life—not when so many relied on his razor-sharp instincts to protect their homes and indeed their lives.

He prided himself on always being able to separate his personal and professional life—especially when it came to affairs with women. Lust never clouded his judgement.

The women he pursued were usually professional workaholics, just like him. Women who were sophisticated in and out of the bedroom and who weren't looking for sweet nothings to be whispered in their ear once they had scratched their mutual itch.

He had a feeling a sheltered young princess wouldn't be quite so worldly when it came to no-strings sex.

He picked up speed as he chastised himself for even entertaining the thought of a no-strings affair with Olivia. Guilt settled heavily in his chest as he thought of the night before, of the thoughts that had run through his brain as he had openly ogled his best friend's intended bride. *Stupid, weak fool.* The words flew by along with his breath as he exhausted his body with a final punishing sprint.

He had always believed that he deserved punishment for the multitude of sins he had committed in his youth. That no matter how complacent he grew in his wealth, in his power and success, there was always a darkness in him just waiting to ruin everything. It was beginning to seem that Olivia had been sent into his life to tempt that darkness to the fore. To tease him with her elegant curves and squeaky-clean nature.

He had a certain code for how he lived his life—certain people he did not betray and certain things he did not do. A rule book, of sorts, that kept him on the straight and narrow when the impulsive bastard inside him threatened to rise to the surface.

Khristos...

He exhaled hard. He had never been more tempted to break his own rules than in these past two days. Olivia reminded him of one of those perfect, luscious cakes that had always been on display behind the glass of his local bakery as a child. He had stood outside in the cold, salivating over the idea of breaking through that glass and claiming the treat for himself. But at that stage in his life his innocent boyhood self had innately known that would have been the wrong thing to do.

The Roman Lazarov of the present day did not have that luxury. Telling himself to walk away last night had been like standing in front of that bakery window all over again—hungry and frustrated, but unable to do a damn thing but fantasise about how the icing would taste in his mouth.

A delicious torture.

With his breath hard and even, he turned to the horizon and watched as the first flickers of pink and orange began to colour the dawn sky.

One of his favourite things about Isla Arista was the unspoilt view of both the sunrise and sunset from various points on the island. In those few dark months after the tragedy in Zayyar he had often spent an entire day walking here. He could completely circumnavigate the island in a few short hours because he knew the right tracks to take. It was an island of many personalities—smooth and habitable in some places, but fiercely wild and impassable in others.

He turned to begin walking back up to the villa, stopping as he spied a familiar feminine silhouette emerge from the open glass doors onto the terrace.

Olivia had been unashamedly watching Roman's progress up and down the beach with interest. It had been impossble not to stare at his broad, muscular form as he powered up and down the sand with seeming effortlessness.

She had debated hiding in her room all day, and avoiding breakfast with him altogether, but she'd decided that was something the *old* Olivia would do.

She was done with avoiding conflict and simply daydreaming of what she might say if she had the bravery in certain situations. She would sit across the table from him this morning and she would show him how completely unaffected she was by what had happened last night. Or almost happened, rather.

Aside from wanting to prove a point to herself, she had to admit that she desperately wanted to speak with him again. He was so unlike any man she had ever known. It was addictive, talking to him.

She had possibly taken slightly more time than usual in washing and preparing her hair, so that it fell in soft waves around her face. And so what if she had tried on three of the five dresses in her suitcase before committing to one?

The pale pink linen day dress was perhaps a little much for breakfast, but the way it nipped in at the waist and flowed out softly to her knees made her feel feminine and confident. And besides, she was simply taking pleasure in choosing her own outfit without a styling team surrounding her.

After twenty minutes of waiting, her stomach rumbling, with a beautiful display of fresh fruit and pastries spread out before her on the breakfast table, Jorge informed her that Mr Lazarov would be working all day and had decided it was easier to eat in his office.

She told herself that she wasn't bothered in the least as she poured herself coffee from the French press and nibbled on a piece of melon. She didn't care that he had chosen to avoid her. It was better, really. There was no one here to goad her, to push her to think about things she wanted to avoid. No all too perceptive slate-grey eyes watching her, making her skin prickle.

Eventually she gave in to the tantalising breakfast display and grabbed a large sugar-frosted croissant, smearing it liberally with butter and strawberry marmalade. The sticky sweet treat was like heaven itself as she washed it down with the fragrant gourmet coffee. Pastry was firmly on her list of *never* foods.

Regret was inevitable, and it washed over her as she self-consciously smoothed her dress against her stomach. Another result of the life she led was the constant pressure to stay slim, to stay as beautiful as possible in order to live up to her persona.

She had always harboured a soul-deep envy of her sisters and their seeming lack of pressure to play a part for the public. As the oldest, Eleanor was to be Queen one day—a position she took very seriously. She was naturally rake-thin, and always immaculately dressed, but the only media pressure *she* had to deal with was speculation on when she would start producing little heirs of her own.

Cressida was rarely, if ever, seen in the media. As a respected researcher in her field, she had somehow been allowed to study and live an almost civilian lifestyle in London, with only the barest minimum security detail.

Olivia sighed. The only skills *she* had were those best suited to what she was already doing, along with the uncanny ability to daydream herself out of any situation.

She had always adored the more dramatic movies—the ones where the heroine went through hell in order to get her happy ending. Maybe this was her punishment for refusing to adapt fully to real life?

Now, the information that lay inside that folder up in her room had the potential to change her life. To give her a little of the freedom she had longed for, for the past ten years. But, as with every choice, there would be some fall-out. And that fall-out would affect the people of her kingdom for many years to come.

Roman had said that she was spoilt and selfish. If that were true then she would have simply walked away from her place in the royal family as soon as she'd legally become an adult. Or when she had been made aware of her private inheritance three years ago.

It was her 'Get Out of Jail Free' card—a golden ticket to civilian life. But she was a royal of the realm at heart, and her father knew that. Hence why he so easily used her own loyal nature against her and made sure that she knew the consequences of her actions if she were to defy him.

She knew her father spoke the truth when he said that this marriage had the potential to solve all of Monteverre's problems.

Could she really be the person to stand in the way of that?

CHAPTER SIX

OLIVIA SAT UP quickly in the bed, feeling a sharp pain shoot through her neck. In her exhausted state she must have fallen asleep with her head propped on one arm. A quick look in the mirror showed that not only was her hair an unsightly nest, but she also bore a hot red patch on her left cheek from her uncomfortable position.

She stood up and walked to windows. A silvery moon had risen high above the bay below, casting pretty shadows all along the gardens that surrounded the villa. It was certainly past dinner time, she imagined, but still her eyes widened as the clock showed it was almost midnight.

Disorientated and groggy, she quickly ran a brush through her hair before making her way downstairs.

The villa seemed to be completely empty, and devoid of all human presence. The air was cool out on the terrace, and she half wished she had thought to take a sweater. From her vantage point she had a spectacular view of the glass-fronted villa in all its warm, glowing glory. At night, somehow the place seemed even more beautiful than it was during the day. Soft lighting warmed the space from within and made it look like a wall of glowing amber stone.

The garden was lit up with small spherical lights that appeared to float in mid-air. Tall, thick shrubbery blocked her view of the moon and its hypnotising glow on the waves. She was filled with energy, and suddenly wanted nothing more than a brisk walk along the moonlit beach.

As she made her way towards the edge of the lights she paused, briefly wondering if it was wise to venture away from the villa. The island was completely private, so she felt she was in no real danger so long as she kept to the well-lit parts. But that didn't mean that her brooding guard would take kindly to her exploring without permission...

That thought was immediately banished once she remembered how her host had effectively barricaded himself in his office for the day. She hadn't so much as caught a glimpse of him since seeing him running on the beach.

Her arms instinctively wrapped around her midriff, shielding herself from both the cool breeze and her thoughts as she made her way down the steps to the beach. Who the hell did he think he was anyway? Did he think that she would shadow him around? Begging for his attention?

She had much more pressing things on her mind than brooding Russians with ridiculously inflated egos.

The steps at the back of the house were steeper than she had anticipated. The drive up in the Jeep had not truly given her an appreciation of how high up the house was perched above the marina. She momentarily considered turning back, but stubbornness and curiosity made her keep moving. There was a safety rail on each side, and small lamps to light the way—it was not truly dangerous.

The soles of her sandals slid suddenly against the stone surface, making her gasp as she teetered forward precariously. The world seemed to shift for a split second before she clambered back, grabbing the rail for dear life.

She slid off her sandals, abandoning them on the steps. Her bare feet gave much better grip for the rest of the way down, and soon she reached the very bottom. The sand was cold and damp under her toes but the midnight air was balmy. She took a moment to stop and simply bask in the utter stillness of it all.

It reminded her of the warm nights her family had spent out on the terrace at their summer estate. The beautiful countryside manor in the southern peninsula of Monteverre was the setting of most of her fondest childhood memories. Back in the days when her grandmother had reigned over the kingdom as

Queen and her father had simply been the young, handsome heir to the throne.

There had been no palace for the three young Princesses—no twenty-four-hour bodyguards. Her grandmother had ensured they were given as normal a childhood as possible, considering the circumstances.

And even as father had grown ever more reckless, and her mother had retreated into her brandy glass, Mimi had been there. Until all of a sudden she hadn't.

Olivia shivered, taking a few long strides across the sand until she reached the long whitewashed jetty of the small marina that she had arrived at. It looked different in the semi-dark, with only a few lamps illuminating the shadows. Roman's sleek yacht was a dark shadow in the distance. The moonlight glowed against its polished glass body, smooth, severe and striking—rather like the man himself, she thought.

The marina also housed a handful of other vessels. A couple of top-of-the-range speedboats—likely for sporting use—a small rescue dinghy, and the one that had caught her eye the moment she had disembarked the day before: a magnificent vintage sailboat.

In the dark, it was hard to see any of the fine detailing. She reached out, running her hand along the smooth silver lettering emblazoned just above the waterline.

"'Sofiya",' she said out loud. 'Just who are you named after, I wonder?'

'That is none of your business.'

The deep voice boomed from behind her, startling her enough to make her lose her footing and fall hard against the side of the boat. She fell for what seemed like minutes rather than milliseconds, before strong arms grabbed her around the waist and lifted her swiftly upright.

'Planning a midnight escape?' Roman asked, his accent both intimidating and strangely welcoming after the prolonged silence of her day.

'You…you startled me,' she breathed hard, her voice little more than a breathy whisper.

His hands were still on her waist, the heat of him seeping through the material of her dress. She reached down, covering his hands with her own for a moment before pushing them away and taking a tentative half-step back.

The loss of heat was instant. Her skin prickled with tiny bumps, as though calling his touch back.

'If you insist on sneaking around outside in the dark, I might rethink the terms of your stay here.'

'The *terms*? I assumed I had been abandoned to my own devices.'

'Fine, then. Let's get this straight. You will only leave the house in daylight hours, and you will clear it with me first.'

'You expect me to just sit around all day and go

insane from my own thoughts?' She half laughed. 'This is an island—where could I even go?'

'I have learnt not to underestimate you.'

He crossed his arms and for the first time she noticed he wore only a dark-coloured sleeveless workout shirt and cut-off shorts. Her eyes took in the bulging muscles that lined his shoulders, his lean, hard biceps and strong forearms. Her gaze wandered once again to the strange black band that stretched around his left arm, just under the elbow. The design seemed intricate, but she quickly looked back up to his face, aware she had been gawking.

'Are we clear?' he asked, scowling down at her from his impressive height.

Olivia fought the urge to roll her eyes at him in all his perpetually sardonic glory. She had a feeling this was what it would be like to have a surly, unimpressed guardian angel following her every move.

In this light he certainly looked the part. The glow of the moon emphasised his harsh features, making him even more darkly attractive. But good looks and incredibly broad shoulders would never account for a severe lack of sense of humour. Did the man *ever* smile?

'Are you like this all the time or just around me?' she asked, turning on her heel and walking away from him, back towards the sand.

'Oh, you're telling me how I am now?' He fell

easily into step beside her, mild amusement on his voice. 'Please enlighten me.'

'You are controlling. And rude.' She said, counting off on her fingers. 'Judgmental, intimidating, far too serious—'

'You are accusing *me* of being rude?' He clutched a hand to his chest as though mortally wounded.

Olivia stopped just short of where the wooden planks gave way to hard sand and turned to face him in the dim light of the spherical lamps that lined the small marina. 'You've just instructed me that I cannot leave the house without your permission.'

He smirked, reaching out to stop her when she made to move away with irritation.

She crossed her arms and met his eyes, determined to have this conversation like an adult.

'Olivia, closely controlled security is only required if there is a risk of the client putting themselves in danger. Unfortunately for me, in your case, that means, yes, it's needed.' He sighed. 'And I am not prepared to shadow you around this island simply to provide you with a more enjoyable experience.'

'Are you telling me I'm under house arrest just because you're determined not to spend any time alone with me?' she said with disbelief.

'I don't think it would be the best idea,' he said plainly. 'For obvious reasons.'

She watched him silently for a moment, wondering if he was actually openly referring to the chemistry between them. 'Are you really so unable to control a flimsy attraction?' she asked bravely, shocked at the words coming from her own mouth.

His eyes widened. 'I'm a grown man, Olivia. Older than you by almost a decade.'

'I fail to see what age has to do with it.'

He stepped forward, a dangerous glint in his slate-grey eyes. 'I'm not a mindless teenager who can be waylaid by a set of curves.'

'Well, then, what's the problem?' She shrugged one shoulder, fully committed to her act now, even as her insides quaked. 'I'm not about to jump your bones, and you've made it clear that you are far too mature to do anything quite so...*primal.*'

He smiled the kind of smile that screamed danger as he allowed his gaze to take her in slowly from her head down to her bare toes. 'Primal? Is that what you'd call it?'

She gulped.

He noticed.

Roman took a single step forward, closing the gap between them so that they stood almost toe to toe. 'I'd like to wager that you've never jumped anyone's bones in your life, Printsessa.'

'I'm not about to divulge that kind of information to you.' She tried her best to keep up her confident act but he'd rattled her. He knew it too.

Cursing her lack of practice in these things, she

turned as nonchalantly as possible and began walking back towards the villa, hoping she'd simply seem bored or tired.

'I did not mean to offend you.' His voice drifted from behind her as she began climbing the steep steps. 'I'm sure you are perfectly capable of jumping my bones.'

'Don't flatter yourself,' she breathed, aware that she was barely a quarter of the way up and already feeling winded from the incline.

She hadn't eaten nearly enough today to fuel this kind of exertion, and tiny spots had begun to appear at the edges of her vision. She paused, holding on to the rail for a moment as she caught her breath.

'Problem?' he asked, coming to a stop beside her.

He was barely even breathing heavily, the great brute.

She shook her head, not wanting to admit that she had been moping around the villa for most of the day and had refused Jorge's offers of lunch and dinner.

Standing up straight, she continued to climb, begging the gods of never-ending stairs to have mercy on her. Eventually she reached the top—and not a moment too soon. She caught one glimpse of the amber lights of the villa before her ears began to pop and her legs started to shake.

Roman instantly noticed the change in her demeanour. 'Was the climb *really* so tough?' he asked, half mocking.

She groaned, moving to the grass and half sitting half falling onto her rear end with an unceremonious grunt as the world tilted around her.

'You look as though you are about to be ill.' He crouched in front of her, the mocking tone completely vanished from his voice. 'Olivia?'

'I need some water,' she managed to rasp, looking up at the blurred outline of his face. 'Just a little light-headed.'

Roman took one look at Olivia's pale features and cursed under his breath. 'When did you last eat?' he asked, a mixture of anger and concern filling him as her eyes darted away from him with embarrassment.

'Just give me a moment to catch my breath.'

'No, you need a damned sandwich and some common sense,' he gritted. 'Can you walk?'

She nodded—far too quickly. Her eyes were still unfocused and her face pale as moonlight. Still, to her stubborn credit she rose to her feet and attempted two whole steps before her legs buckled and she tipped into his waiting arms.

'This is mortifying!' she groaned, her face mashed against his chest.

Roman ignored the all too welcome sensation of having her slim figure pressed against him. With a deep breath he lifted her against his shoulder and closed the distance between them and the villa.

Once inside, he deposited her roughly onto the

bench in the kitchen and set about preparing a cold meat sandwich on crusty white bread and a tall glass of ice-cold orange juice.

She sipped at the juice with gusto, and a hint of colour reappeared in her cheeks after a moment as she nibbled on the crust of the bread.

'You eat like a rabbit,' he commented, when after five minutes she hadn't taken more than a series of tiny bites.

'I eat enough.' She shrugged.

Roman remained silent. She was watching him closely over the rim of her orange juice glass, but did not speak until the sandwich was completely gone.

'White carbs are my weakness.' She sighed. 'You've just sent me down a path of total and utter ruination in the eyes of my stylist.'

'I'm sorry its not gluten-free, but true hunger can't afford to be picky.'

'What would *you* know of true hunger?' She raised a brow. 'You eat enough to feed a small army.'

'I grew accustomed to eating as much as I could fit in once I got out of prison.' He spoke without thought, and then watched as stark realisation dawned over her delicate features. 'Old habits, I suppose.' He shrugged, instantly regretting his words.

'I never thought…' She let her voice trail off. 'I'm sorry.'

'You're sorry that I was in prison?' He leaned down, grabbing her plate and turning to deposit it in the sink. 'Don't be. I deserved every year I got. Trust me.'

'No, I'm sorry you had to experience hunger like that. I didn't think when I spoke. I was just being… snarky.'

'Don't worry about it.'

In all the years that had passed since his time in jail, he couldn't remember anyone ever commiserating with him over the hardships he must have endured. She didn't even know why he had been landed there in the first place. She knew nothing of the man he had been. No, he corrected himself, the *boy* he had been.

'You're not a bad guy,' she said quietly.

Roman looked up, unable to conceal his surprise at her words.

'I mean, obviously I've only known you a couple of days…' She shrugged her shoulders, heat lightly warming her cheeks. 'But a bad guy wouldn't have brought me here to begin with. He wouldn't be making sandwiches at one in the morning to stop me from fainting like a helpless damsel.'

'Don't paint me as some hero, Olivia.' He shook his head. 'You have no idea how far that is from the truth.'

She made to continue talking, but he'd suddenly had enough. He put a hand up, silencing her. 'I've had a long day, and I'd appreciate it if you considered what I said about obeying my rules tomorrow.'

'I'll consider it.'

She shrugged, then walked past him into the hallway and began ascending the stairs, effectively robbing him of the chance to walk away first.

'That didn't sound like a yes.' He sighed, trying and failing to avoid the delectable sight of her shapely bare calves below the hemline of her dress.

'That's because it wasn't one.'

She disappeared from his view.

Olivia shielded her eyes as her hair whipped around her. The wind was like razor blades at this altitude, but the hour-long hike had definitely been worth it. She braced herself, taking one step out onto the balcony of the lighthouse. Heights had never really been an issue for her, but then again she had never been alone on a ledge in coastal winds before.

But all fear was forgotten once she stepped out and felt the sun spread across her face, warming her through.

There was nothing but ocean ahead of her for miles. She turned and caught her breath. She could see the entire island in all its glowing emerald glory. A heavy sigh escaped her lips and she leaned her elbows against the metal railing.

The villa was little more than a pea-sized white blur from here, partially hidden in the trees far over to the north. Likely Roman was still holed up in his office there, determined to spend as little time in her company as possible.

She had almost been tempted to go and ask him to show her the lighthouse. She had walked boldly up to his office door and stood poised, ready to knock. But then she had remembered his face as he'd called her Princess. The patronising tone as he had all but called her a child in need of supervision. She had not actually agreed to his terms, so technically she wasn't breaking any promises.

The hike had been just what she'd needed to shake off the extra energy that had plagued her all morning. She had made a point of eating a good wholesome breakfast before setting off, not wanting to make the same mistake as she had the night before. Now her thighs burned from exertion and her cheeks were warm and she finally felt as if she was *doing* something. And the best part of all was that she was entirely alone.

A harsh male roar caught her by surprise and her hand almost slipped on the railing. She looked down, wide-eyed, and caught sight of Roman powering across the plane at the base of the lighthouse, angry determination in his posture as he stopped and looked up at her.

He shouted something entirely inaudible, his voice fighting against the noise of the wind and the waves below. Olivia couldn't help it—she laughed. The smile that erupted on her lips made him scowl even more as he powered ahead once more and disappeared through the door beneath her.

There were at least three storeys between them, made up of one long winding staircase, and yet it seemed like barely a minute passed before she heard him step out onto the platform behind her.

'What the hell do you think you're doing up here?' he growled.

Olivia turned to look at him over her shoulder. 'I'm enjoying the view.'

'Oh, of course. Of *course* you'd have to perch yourself fifty feet in the air. You couldn't just stand on the deck below like a normal person.'

'The door was unlocked and I've never seen the inside of a lighthouse before.' She shrugged, holding onto the railing to pull herself up. 'It's not half as quaint as I'd imagined.'

She turned to face Roman, seeing his look of cold rage turn quickly to disbelief.

'This isn't a game, Olivia,' he said darkly. 'What if you'd fallen?'

'I'm quite capable of using stairs without supervision.' She stood tall, wishing he wouldn't keep looking at her that way. 'Please, just…stop treating me like a child.'

'Well, then, stop acting like one!' He raised his voice.

She sidestepped him, neatly sliding through the doorway and starting down the steps at a rapid pace.

He followed quickly behind her.

'You are the most reckless, difficult client I have ever had.' Roman stalked behind her, his voice still holding that dark edge.

'Because I wanted to explore a little?' She paused, turning to look back at him. 'This entire island is more secure than the royal vaults. You knew exactly where I was—as evidenced by the fact that you are *here*.'

'I was at least ten minutes behind you.'

'You are seriously overreacting, and I would like to know why.'

He met her eyes easily, his height making him tower above her even more than usual. 'I'm reacting as anyone would if they found the woman they are supposed to be protecting dangling her legs from a fifty-foot balcony.'

'It would hardly be your fault if I fell, would it?' She shrugged, turning back to continue down the steps. 'I'm sure your beloved Khal would find a replacement princess eventually.'

Strong hands encased her shoulders, effectively barring her from moving. Roman moved around her so they stood face to face.

She was almost completely level with him on the step below. The expression on his face completely took her breath away.

'Do you honestly have a death wish?' He grasped

her shoulders tightly, his eyes blazing with real, deep concern.

'I... No, of course not.' She turned her face away from him, only for him to turn it right back.

His fingers were hot and hard against her cheek, and this close she was surrounded by the warm, delicious aroma of him that she had come to recognise so well.

'Your eyes tell me a different story.'

'Isn't that against the rules? Looking into my eyes?'

Was that her voice? That husky murmur? She could feel her heart hammering hard and slow in her chest. It was as though the simple act of being near him sent her vitals into chaos.

'I've always hated rules.'

His mouth tightened, and tension spread through his hands and up his arms so that they felt like bands of iron on her shoulders rather than flesh and bone.

She bit her bottom lip as shivers spread down her arms. Roman's eyes lowered to take in the movement, his pupils darkening as he pressed his lips together hard. She thought he might kiss her. He certainly looked as though he wanted to.

But she saw the moment that something changed in his eyes—something that made his mouth harden and his eyes shift away from her once more.

For one crazy moment she wondered what it might be like to lean across and kiss all that tension from his mouth. To just take a wild leap and not care about the consequences.

And then all of a sudden she was doing it.

She closed the gap between them and laid her mouth against his, feeling his shocked intake of breath as their lips connected and her breasts pressed flush against the hard, strong plane of his chest.

He was going to hell.

There were no two ways about it.

Roman felt something inside him roar to life the moment Olivia's lips gently touched his, her feather-light caresses against his mouth almost completely undoing him. His hands found their way to her hair, releasing the clasp that held it wound at the nape of her neck.

He was letting this happen.

More than that, he wanted it so badly it made him ache.

She gave just as good as she got, her hands travelling over his shoulders and down his waist. Sharp fingernails grasped his hips just above his jeans. The sensation sent pulses of heat southwards and he felt himself grow hard against his zip.

The fleeting thought of stopping the madness came and went quickly as Olivia moved against him, her abdomen in direct contact with his erection. Far from being shocked or appalled, she kissed him even harder.

Their breath mingled into one frantic cloud of white-hot need. He kissed a trail down her neck, his hands sweeping deftly to the front closures of her blouse. With each satisfying click he was treated to a delicious sliver of creamy soft skin and the smallest glimpse of white lace.

Her breasts were small and firm, perfectly rounded and straining against the lace fabric of her bra. With one hand he reached behind her, undoing the clasp.

She exhaled long and slow, biting her lip as he pulled the garment away and lowered his mouth to her breast. Her skin tasted like a smooth ripe peach, the softness unbelievable against his tongue.

As he drew one peak into his mouth she hissed out a breath. 'Roman…' she breathed in awe.

Her fingers wound through his hair, anchoring him to her as he explored one taut peak and then gave ample attention to the other.

Their position on the steps made things difficult. It would be so easy to carry her down to the landing below and take her hard and fast on the floor. He could tell she was ready for him by the way she moaned at the slightest touch. She was his for the taking…

Except, she wasn't, was she?

The thought stilled him, stopping his body mid-motion.

She wasn't his.

Roman stepped away from her as though he'd been burned. His breath escaped his nostrils in harsh bursts as his body screamed in protest. He cursed out loud, his voice echoing in the cavernous space as he realised what he had been doing. What his body was still deeply invested in doing.

Olivia fell back at an uncomfortable angle, her breasts still bared to him. She looked up, confused and flushed.

'That shouldn't have happened,' he breathed, bracing his back against the cold wall and forcing himself to look away from the tantalising curves on display.

In his peripheral vision he saw Olivia stiffen, her hands quickly moving to cover herself. A prolonged silence ensued as he turned his back and listened while she frantically tried to button up her blouse and calm her breathing. When he finally turned around it was to find her gone—back up the stairs to the top of the lighthouse.

He followed, stepping out soundlessly onto the narrow balcony alongside her.

'Olivia…' he began, exhaling on a long sigh.

'Whatever you are about to say, just *don't*,' she said, her voice tight with recrimination and something else—regret, perhaps?

'It won't happen again, between us,' he said, almost as though he were trying to convince himself along with her. 'It was a mistake, bringing you here at all. This just proves what I already knew.'

'And that is?'

'That you are incapable of controlling your impulses.'

'And *you* are the most arrogant man I have ever met.' She turned to face him. 'Are you actually trying to blame *me* for this?' she asked. 'I may have kissed you first, but at least I'm emotionally mature enough to admit it was because I wanted it.'

'Excuse me?'

'I wanted it.' She spoke slowly and deliberately, her eyes blazing emerald in the brightness of the mid-afternoon sun. 'I wanted to know how it would feel, being kissed by you. To get under that wall of stone you surround yourself with. And I may be unpractised in these things, but I know that you wanted it too.'

His mind caught on one single word she had uttered. *Unpractised.* He coughed on the sharp intake of breath that filled his lungs.

Olivia's eyes widened, her face rapidly warming with embarrassment. 'I simply meant that I'm not accustomed to making the first move,' she said quickly, her eyes wide with mortification.

'Chert voz'mi,' Roman cursed under his breath, suddenly despising his own ability to see through to the truth. 'You have never had a lover, have you?'

He watched as her shoulders tensed and she tightened her grip on the rail in front of her. She hid her face from him but he could read the signs in her body. Surprise rapidly turned to self-defence. She didn't speak, but she didn't have to. He already knew he was right.

She was a virgin.

As if there weren't enough reasons already for this attraction to be the worst kind of wrong...

He turned, bracing one hand on the balcony rail and gripping it with all his might. 'Have you any idea what kind of game you are playing?' he gritted.

'I was not playing a game.' She turned her face to him, her shoulders stiff and unyielding.

'How would you even *know* what you were doing?' he said harshly. Anger raged in him—towards her, towards himself. He felt as if he was drowning in it. 'What did you think? That you could use me as a damned test run? Lose your virginity with the rough and tumble ex-con before I sent you back to your royal fiancé's bed?'

Her eyes narrowed, her fist flying out to thump him squarely in the middle of his chest. 'How dare you?'

He grabbed her hand in his fist, stopping her movement and inadvertently pulling her closer to him.

'You are angry at me because it is the truth. You

think you are attracted to me? You don't even *know* me. You're attracted to my lack of refinement, Olivia. You see me as some big, uncivilised fool who you can charm with your delicate skin and innocent eye-flutters.' He shook his head, his mouth hardening into a cruel line.

'I don't think of you that way.'

'Well, maybe you should start. I might come from the gutter, but that doesn't mean I make a habit of living like a street thug. I do not sleep with virgins or with other men's fiancées. I have morals, Olivia.'

'What? And I don't? I am not engaged. I have done nothing wrong here.'

'You are as good as spoken for,' he ground out.

She looked up at him. Eyes that moments ago had been blue-black with desire were now wide and blazing with anger. 'I will *never* be spoken for. Never again.' A tremor passed through her throat. 'I am not another man's property, to be protected and transported.'

'You are going back to the palace as soon as possible.'

'Roman, is it so hard to believe that I am just as overwhelmed as you?'

'Don't flatter yourself, Princess,' he said cruelly. 'It would take a lot more than an innocent's clumsy kisses to overwhelm *me*.'

Her face fell and he knew he had gone too far.

But she was already turning to walk out through

the door. 'If you don't mind, I'd like to walk back alone.'

He made to walk after her but stopped, thinking it might be best if they both had some time to calm down.

'Fine. You can take the time to prepare your explanation. I will deliver you to your fiancé tonight.'

CHAPTER SEVEN

Olivia regretted stealing Roman's boat almost as soon as she had set off, but stubbornness kept her from turning back. As the wind pulled her hair around her face and the salty air filled her lungs she felt the awful tension inside her loosen a fraction.

She hated him.

Every single word that Roman had thrown at her had swum around in her head as she had hiked across the craggy woodland towards the villa. His indignant accusations. His refusal to see the truth in their situation. He seemed determined to power through any argument she had.

It was the thought of his final words that had cemented her decision to change course and hightail it for the marina. *'I will deliver you to your fiancé tonight.'*

She gripped the wheel even tighter, steering the boat as the mainland drew nearer on the horizon. The distance between Isla Arista and the small mainland town of Puerto Arista was a mere fifteen minutes, but as the small dock came into view she contemplated turning around.

What *was* it about her breaking the law when she was around this man? Once again she had proved him right by giving in to an emotional impulse without a thought for the consequences.

Still, pride kept her from doing the intelligent thing and returning with her tail between her legs. She busied herself with mooring and disembarking safely, taking pleasure in the manual work.

She had always enjoyed her national sport—there was something quite peaceful about letting her mind wander as she followed through all the steps.

This small speedboat was much more streamlined and modern than the complex sporting sailboats she was used to, so before she knew it she was climbing the limestone steps up from the dock and emerging into a busy little Spanish village. Thankfully she had worn large sunglasses and a floppy-brimmed hat on her hike, to protect her from the sun, both of which now helpfully concealed her face from possible recognition.

The streets were cobbled and sloped upwards towards the impressive white cliffs that dominated the landscape. A long row of whitewashed houses and shops lined the seafront, with terracotta roofs and vibrantly coloured windows. The village was small, and seemed almost pristine in its appearance.

It was quiet. There was none of the hustle and

bustle of the coastal spots in Monteverre. It was like stepping into a well-kept secret. People smiled as they walked past, shopkeepers tipped their sunhats in her direction. No one approached her or called her name. No one cared.

It was a revelation.

After she had walked to the top of the hill and back down her stomach began to growl. The thought of returning to the island—to Roman—filled her with trepidation. Without a second thought she walked into a nearby café and eyed the delicious selection of handmade pastries and freshly cut fruit. The smell of warm butter and melted chocolate permeated the air and made her stomach flip.

Yes, this was exactly what she needed.

'Can I help you, miss?' A middle-aged man smiled jovially from behind the counter, his white apron smeared with powdered sugar.

Olivia smiled in response, really enjoying not being recognised. 'Yes—what's good here?'

'It's all good, of course.' He laughed. 'We have a special on today: three *magdalenas* for the price of two.'

Olivia looked down at the elegant golden-brown pastries and instantly felt her stomach drop.

She had no money.

With a murmured excuse she practically ran from the shop, embarrassment fuelling her as she walked swiftly down the hill back towards the marina. She stopped on the promenade, taking a seat on a bench that overlooked the small inlet.

As her breathing slowed, a heavy sadness replaced her embarrassment. She had no idea how to prepare for living in the real world. For all her thoughts of leaving her bubble and making a difference, the reality was that she had absolutely no idea how to function outside the privilege of royal life.

Her father had been right.

She had told herself that she would find a way to become the woman she wanted to be outside of her parents' expectations and royal obligations. She had believed she could fulfil the vision her grandmother had had for the foundation alone. But she didn't have a business mind—she didn't have that kind of common sense or leadership skill. She certainly didn't have the kind of innate intelligence and passion that could support her, as her siblings did.

Maybe she was delusional. Maybe her father was right and she should stick to where her strengths lay. Just another Sandoval princess, destined to stand and smile by her husband's side.

But one thing was for sure: she was *not* what Roman had accused her of being. She had not seen him as some sort of base creature to use for her own amusement. The thought that he saw her as someone capable of such cruelty…it bothered her.

She ambled towards the marina with the intention of returning and paused, watching as a familiar sailboat moored itself next to her smaller vessel. The name *Sofiya* was emblazoned across its hull.

Roman jumped down athletically onto the boards of the jetty before striding purposefully in her direction.

She turned away quickly, not quite ready for the confrontation she knew was bound to happen. He was likely furious, and he had every right to be. But she had hoped for more time to compose herself before the inevitable. Even now, the memory of his hands on her bare skin made her short of breath.

She shook off the heated thoughts, walking along the promenade at a brisk pace.

A man was walking towards her—the man from the pastry shop, she realised suddenly. He was walking quite fast and had a slightly odd expression on his face. Olivia paused, feeling suddenly very exposed on the empty promenade. As he neared her he reached into his jacket, his large hand fumbling for something in his breast pocket.

A loud growl erupted from somewhere over her left shoulder. Roman was running past her in a matter of seconds, moving to stand in front of the older man with ferocious agility and strength. His large body manoeuvred the man to the ground and he shouted to Olivia to move away. She could hear the man calling out underneath him—a strange muffled cry of one word, over and over.

Finally Roman moved from his position and the other man managed to gasp. 'Camera! Camera!'

Olivia spied the small black object that lay shattered near Roman's left knee. She rushed forward. 'Roman, it's just a camera!' She gasped, tugging at his sleeve for his to remove his body from the man. 'Roman, please stand up. He's not dangerous,' she urged, pulling at his shoulder.

Roman looked into the blue-green depths of Olivia's eyes and something inside him shifted. All at once he became aware of the man's fleshy paunch beside his knee. The roar of the waves hitting the promenade to his left. He could hear Olivia's panicked tone and his own fiercely ragged breathing.

Khristos, it had happened again.

He stood to his feet, looking away from where his unsuspecting, seemingly innocent victim had stood up and shuffled away. The roaring in his ears was deafening, the hammering in his chest making him feel as though he might pass out.

Without thinking of the lack of logic in his actions, he grabbed Olivia roughly by the wrist, ignoring her protests. Eventually she gave in and allowed him to lead her down to where his sailboat lay in wait. Within moments they were on board, and he closed the door of the spacious interior saloon with a harsh exhalation of breath.

'Sit down,' he commanded, watching confusion enter into her eyes.

'Roman, what on earth—?'

'Just sit down,' he repeated harshly, his breath still raw and uneven in his chest as he fought to control the ridiculous racing of his treacherous mind.

Sofiya.

His mind whirled against the onslaught of terrible memories threatening to overcome him as his sister's face broke through to his consciousness. As if in slow motion he could see the life leave her baby-blue eyes as the bullet tore through her body, silencing her scream.

He shook his head, swallowing past the dryness of fear in his throat.

Olivia moved in front of him, concern in her wide eyes as she placed her hands on his chest.

'You're shaking,' she said softly, in the kind of placating tone one used when trying to soothe a wild animal. 'Has this happened before?'

Her warm hands on his chest both irritated and calmed him. 'Don't push me, Olivia,' he warned. 'I don't want to hurt you, too.'

'You won't hurt me, Roman.'

She shook her head just a fraction, her innocent eyes so wide and confused it made him want to growl with frustration and bask in her concern all at once.

'Let me help you,' she whispered, moving her hand uncertainly to rest on his face.

The touch of her soft, feminine hands on his skin undid him completely.

He leaned forward, capturing her words roughly with his mouth, showing her just why she needed to run from him.

Her lips were soft against his, trying in vain to offer him comfort even as he plundered and deepened the kiss. He wound one hand around the back of her neck and twisted the fine silk of her hair in his hands. His rough touch anchored her to him while his other hand bunched into a tight fist by his side.

This was wrong, he told himself. He was using her in the aftermath of his own weakness, losing himself in her, and it was so wrong he hated himself. She was innocent to situations like this, he reminded himself, talking himself down from his own madness. She deserved better than this—than him.

He moved to away an inch and she looked up at him, lust clouding her vision.

'I can't keep my hands off of you,' he gritted, running his fingers down one side of her face and wincing as he noticed the small patch of blood staining the front of her dress.

Logic told him that the blood was likely from his own cut knuckles, but the sight of her pale skin next to the red smear was enough to sober him just for a moment. He tried to fish though the haze of his memory but drew up nothing but blankness.

'Roman, I need to know what happened back

there.' She spoke slowly, as though afraid she might set him off again.

'I don't want to talk right now.' He shook his head, pulling himself away from the heat of her, inch by inch, even as his body screamed in protest.

It was colder without her in his arms, but safer.

'Talk to me,' she said simply.

'I'm not good at talking, Olivia.' He turned to sit heavily on the leather sofa of the saloon. 'Guns trigger something inside me. Even the *thought* of guns, apparently.' He laughed cruelly.

'There was no gun, Roman,' she said. 'No danger.'

He stood, his anger boiling over to the surface. 'You think I don't *know* that?' he asked. 'But in that moment, when my mind goes there…'

'You are powerless to stop it?' she offered helpfully.

Powerless. God, how he hated that term. Was there anything in the world more terrifying than being out of control of your own mind and body, even if only for a few moments?

Olivia moved to sit beside him, her thigh brushing his on the small settee.

'You can talk about it with me, if it helps,' she offered.

'We are not all built for flowery conversations and sharing our dreams.'

Her eyes dropped and he realised he was doing it again—being needlessly cruel.

'None of this would have happened if you hadn't

run off with my damn boat,' he continued, seemingly unable to stop himself.

'You deserved it,' she said harshly.

'For trying to protect your reputation?' he said incredulously.

'I don't think my reputation has a thing to do with it, Roman. You attacked a stranger, dragged me back here like the hounds of hell were chasing you and then you kissed me like your life depended on it.'

She met his eyes without hesitation.

'I kissed you to shut you up,' he argued, turning towards the bridge that housed the control panel so they could get the hell out of here and he could find some space.

'Now who's running away?' she challenged.

'You'd prefer to wait around until local law enforcement arrives to question us both?' he said darkly. 'I didn't even stop to see if I had hurt him.'

'He was fine—just shaken. You don't remember *any* of it?' She frowned. 'I got the chance to apologise quickly before you pulled me away.'

'If you think an apology is enough to stop him from pressing charges...'

'I told him that you were just a jealous lover.' She winced, half smiling with embarrassment.

Roman took a moment to look at her, and the situation suddenly replayed in his mind like a bad movie. He pursed his lips and then, before he knew it, dark laughter erupted from his chest.

Olivia smiled, also seeing the humour in their situation, and soon she was laughing too. She had a great laugh, he thought to himself as they both returned to silence after a moment.

'Thank you,' he said, looking deeply into her eyes for a moment.

He wasn't accustomed to thanking anyone for anything quite so personal; he made a point of not needing anyone enough to necessitate heartfelt apologies. But this woman had lied for him—protected him in a way. After he had treated her horribly.

It was a strange feeling—one he didn't want to examine too closely. For now, the ability to laugh it off was a novelty in itself.

Olivia nodded once—a graceful acceptance.

He took a step away from her, looking out at the harbour around them. It was late; the sky was already in full darkness around them. He suddenly did not want to return to the island—to the silence of the villa and the self-imposed exile he had placed himself in.

'Are you hungry?' he asked hopefully.

Simply named Faro, the small restaurant was partly built into the rocks that stood proudly at the tip of the peninsula. Olivia felt butterflies in her stomach as Roman's hand encircled hers, helping her down the steep steps to the low wooden door of the entrance.

'It doesn't look like much from the outside, but I assure you it's the best paella in all of Spain.'

'I'll take your word for it.'

She smiled, following him into a small hallway. Roman led the way down a corridor and out onto a large terrace that overlooked the coast as far as the eye could see. Warm glowing lanterns adorned the walls and brightened the space, making it seem like the terrace at the back of someone's home rather than a restaurant.

The overall effect was so welcoming she felt instantly at ease, all her tension from the afternoon leaving her shoulders as the waiter led them to a table on the very edge of the space. A man rushed over to take Roman's hand and clap him on the back. The pair began conversing in perfect English, and Roman ordered bottle of red wine.

When it came, Olivia took a sip of her wine, thanking the waiter and looking out across the bay. They were so close to the water she could see the waves crashing into the rocks below them. The after-effects of the day made her forehead tighten painfully.

Roman seemed determined to avoid the subject of their kiss entirely.

Both kisses.

She shivered at the memory of his rough handling after he had all but dragged her back to his boat. He had been completely raw and out of control, and yet she had felt nothing but excitement. Maybe he was right—maybe she *was* just looking for a taste of danger. Maybe she was naïve for not fearing him.

He had made one thing clear: he did not trust her. She desperately wanted to ask him about the incident on the promenade—find out why a man who ran a company of armed bodyguards would have such a deep issue with guns. But maybe she was a fool for worrying about him when he'd continuously told her she was no more than a job to him.

She had told him that she was a virgin and he had made it clear that the fact only cemented his view of her as being completely untouchable. She had never resented her own pesky innocence more than at that moment. When had he stopped being just a glowering bodyguard and become the object of all her fantasies?

She swallowed hard past the dryness in her throat as Roman sat down across from her and apologised for the interruption. After checking with her first, he ordered them both a light starter followed by the chef's special paella.

Once the waiter had taken their order they were left completely alone. The moment of uncomfortable silence was not lost on Olivia. She cleared her throat, making a show of looking up at the vaulted ceiling that partially covered the open terrace.

'You seem to know the staff quite well,' she offered.

'It's been five years, I believe, since I started coming here for lunch every day when I was overseeing building work on my island.'

'They seem to like you.'

'The chef—he is also the owner. And the waiters are his sons.' He smiled, looking over at the young men bustling around the small restaurant. 'The first day I found this place, my architect brought me for lunch. The owner, Pedro, had an argument with his oldest boy and the kid ran off, leaving him with a pile of dishes and a line of hungry guests. I rolled up my sleeves and offered to help.'

'Not many people would do that.'

'Not many princesses would do what you did at that racetrack.' Roman shrugged, sitting back as their bread and gazpacho were laid out on their table.

Olivia couldn't mask her surprise at his mention of the incident with the young waiter and the champagne. 'That afternoon seems like a lifetime ago.'

He nodded. 'Perhaps we are both destined for the sainthood?'

She smiled. 'If you are hoping to convince me that you are not entirely heartless, it's working.'

'I might not have the benevolent influence of a royal, but I'm not afraid to get my hands dirty.' He shrugged again. 'Charity isn't always about money.'

'That's…' She shook her head, frowning at the memory of her argument with her father. Of those very words that she had spoken so vehemently. And here was Roman, echoing them as though it were simply a fact.

'Is something wrong?' he asked, frowning.

She shook her head, ignoring the painful throb in her chest at hearing his words.

She took another sip of wine, clearing the fullness from her throat. 'I adore my work in the community...' Olivia sighed, unable to hide the wistfulness that crept into her voice. 'I swear it's the only time I feel like I'm doing something worthwhile with my life.'

'That sounds like a vocation,' he said, sipping from his own glass. 'And yet you don't sound fulfilled.'

She shook her head. 'This might surprise you, but princesses don't have much sway when it comes to promoting new education laws or increasing expenditure on public schooling.' She sighed again. 'Since the crackdown on my security I've missed several important events. Perhaps the children won't even have noticed. Perhaps I'm only helping *myself* by going out there, boosting my own self-importance. Maybe I'm just an egomaniac.'

'I highly doubt that,' he said, all seriousness. 'This bothers you? Your lack of power?'

'Of course it does. How would *you* feel if you had people holding you back from living your own life at every step?'

A strange look passed over his face, disappearing just as quickly.

'I can only do so much.' She shrugged. 'Potential future innovators of my kingdom are sitting in homeless shelters and all I am allowed to do lately is hold charity balls. It means absolutely *nothing*.'

'Your work means more to those children than you could ever know.'

'How can you know that?'

Roman was quiet for a long time, his hands held tight in front of him. Then, 'I've lived that life. A long time ago, now. But you never forget.' He forced a smile, draining his glass. 'I know that a stranger's kindness means more to a homeless child than you would ever believe.'

Olivia took in the tightness on his features, the guarded emotions in his dark steel-grey eyes. 'Roman, I had no idea...'

'My past is not something that I like to relive. I just want you to know that your work has value. I owe much of my success to men and women I never even knew. They received no thanks, no rewards. I never understood such selfless giving—it was not something I had grown up to feel. Never doubt such honest goodness, Olivia.'

'I am sorry that you had such a difficult upbringing.'

'I'm not. It made me who I am today. But I am not arrogant enough to forget that the world would be an awful place if it was only filled with cynical men like me.'

Olivia understood him then—a little more than before, at least. 'You're not so bad.'

He laughed. 'You don't know the half of it.'

'Tell me, then,' she said quickly. 'Tell me whatever it is you think is so awful about yourself and let me be the judge.'

'Mine is not the kind of story you tell over paella and wine.' The laughter died from his voice, making it clear that the topic was not open for further discussion.

Their main course was laid in front of them, providing a welcome distraction. The food was delicious, and yet as Olivia watched Roman eat she couldn't help but imagine him as a young boy. Thin and hungry…helpless. It was a jarring thought—one that filled her throat with emotion.

She hated to think of anyone suffering through such hardship—especially considering the luxury she had been born into. It had never sat well with her, the enormous divide between the wealthy and the poverty-stricken. She had always felt a weight on her shoulders and an obligation to do her part.

'That was delicious,' she said, forcing a smile as the waiter came to clear their plates and replenish their wine glasses.

'I hope this meal has done something to make up for my behaviour so far,' he said, lowering his glass and looking at her. Sincerity darkened his eyes as he held her gaze. 'For some reason the idea that you see me as cold and cruel bothers me.'

'I don't think you are cold at all,' she said, in all seriousness. 'I think that's just what you prefer people to believe.'

The night had grown cold by the time they embarked at the Puerto Arista harbour and set sail for the short trip back to the island.

Olivia apologised once again for the fact that they had had to abandon his luxury speedboat, but Roman assured her it was fine. They fell into silence as he concentrated on moving the boat along the harbour safely towards open water, each of them deep in thought.

A spark in the sky behind them startled her, and she turned back just in time to see an explosion of red and blue lights erupt into the perfect black sky.

'It must be midnight,' Roman said from behind her.

She could feel him lower their speed and allow the boat to drift slightly.

'This firework display is not one to be missed, trust me.'

'There's no need to stop just for my benefit,' she said quickly.

'Consider it part two of my apology.'

He guided her to the sun deck and pulled two cushions from the built-in sofa, laying them on the cold tiled floor. It was slippery with mist, and just a little chilly, but as a cascade of golden lights began to spread across the inky black sky she knew she wouldn't have changed the night for anything.

After the final booming red spinning wheels had faded into the air, she turned to see he was watching her intently. She took in the heat in his gaze and knew he was battling with the aftermath of that kiss just as she was. She had never wanted to be kissed again more in her life.

'We should be getting back,' he rasped, his eyes not leaving hers.

'I'm really tired of doing what I *should* do all the time.' She licked her lips, silently urging him to give in one more time to the madness between them.

'Olivia…' He shook his head a fraction, lowering his eyes from hers.

She reached out to lay her hand just under the collar of his shirt, knowing she was being brazen but needing to do *something*. To show him in definite terms what her mind was struggling to convey with words.

He took her hand in his, lowered it back to her lap. 'You're not the only one who has to live by the rules,' he said quietly. 'Sometimes they are there to stop us from getting in too deep where we don't belong.'

'I am a grown woman, Roman. If I decide to take a leap into something unknown, you'd better be sure that I've got my reasons.'

'You might *think* you know what you want—'

Olivia stood quickly, looking down at him. 'I told you that I won't be spoken for again,' she warned him, feeling her temper bubble to the surface as she alternated between wanting to hit him and wanting to beg him to take her into his arms.

'Speak, then,' he said plainly, sitting back to look up at her. 'What is it that you want?'

'It's more what I *don't* want,' she said. 'Being here—away from the bubble of royal life—being with you…' She took a breath, urging the words out, needing to say them even if he simply walked away.

Roman shook his head, not giving her a chance to continue as he jumped to his feet and moved back downstairs to start up the engine once more.

The rest of their journey back to the island was silent and tense, unspoken words heavy in the air between them. She wanted to ask him if he still planned to take her back to the palace tomorrow. If he still believed that she should go ahead with the marriage.

The Jeep ride was bumpy, and all too quickly they were standing in the dim empty hallway of the villa. Jorge must have closed up for the night and headed off to his quarters on the opposite side of the island.

'Goodnight, Olivia.'

Roman's voice was dark and final as he made to walk away from her.

'Wait,' she said quietly. 'I've realised something.'

He turned around, crossing his arms over his chest as he waited for her to speak.

Olivia cleared her throat, suddenly feeling very much on show. 'I've realised that I don't want to walk away from my kingdom, and if marrying a stranger is the way to keep it safe then perhaps that's what needs to be done.'

She took a deep breath, wondering if that was relief or disappointment that flickered momentarily across his features. She couldn't tell in the dim hallway.

'You are quite the sacrificial lamb,' he said quietly, with not a hint of emotion in his tone. 'So you plan to return to the palace and accept the marriage?'

'I've decided to return, yes. And face the situation like an adult, at least.' She met his eyes, challenging him in the darkness. 'But I can't fully commit to the marriage knowing there is one thing I have yet to experience in life.'

'I thought you ran away because there were *many* things you hadn't experienced?' he said, sarcasm dripping from his tone.

'There is only one that truly matters to me. I cannot agree to an arranged marriage without allowing myself to experience one of the things I truly have control over.'

His gaze was pure heat as he moistened his lips with one smooth flick of his tongue. She felt heat spread down through her veins and pool in her stomach. If a simple look could make her feel this way, she needed to know what else he could make her feel. It was suddenly the only thing she wanted.

'I want my first time with a man to be on *my* terms, with someone who wants me just as badly as I want him.'

CHAPTER EIGHT

IN HIS MIND Roman simply gathered her into his arms and carried her up to his suite as fast as his legs could take him. Surely this was far more torture than one man was expected to endure? But in reality he remained silent for a long moment, his throat dry as his mind fought to sort between loyalty and lust.

She was offering herself to him on a silver platter.

'You think you can separate sex from love?' he said softly.

'If the sex is good enough.' She shrugged one delicate shoulder, biting her lower lip gently as though embarrassed by her own words.

She couldn't even say the word without blushing and she wanted to fall into bed with him. He took one step towards her, then another, until they were almost toe to toe.

'Men like me don't make love, Olivia,' he said darkly. 'They don't make empty promises just to play into some fantasy.'

She gulped, looking up at him through hooded lashes. 'What if I don't want the fantasy?'

'I have a thousand fantasies I could tell you about,' he whispered. 'Each one more risqué and physically demanding than the last. I would have you naked in my bed quicker than you could beg me to take you. Is that what you want me to say?'

'I...' Her voice trailed off, her eyes wide with uncertainty.

Roman let one finger trace the curve of her shoulder. 'You're not ready for me, Princess,' he said cruelly. 'You need a man who is going to whisper sweet nothings in your ear and make sugar-coated promises. I'm not that man.'

Roman braced his hand on the door of his suite and laid his forehead against the wood—hard.

Loyalty be damned. He wanted nothing more than to break down every door between them and take her like the unrefined street thug that he was.

But she was a virgin. She was not his to take.

Even as his mind thought the words his fist tightened in protest.

He took another deep, rattling breath, feeling the stale air of the room fill his lungs to bursting point.

She was not his.

With more force than necessary he turned and swung open the door to the terrace, silently thanking his housekeeper for placing his guest in the opposite wing of the villa. What would Olivia think of him now? Standing out in the night air, trying desperately to calm his raging libido like a scorned youth?

He looked across to where the light shone out from her rooms.

No. He shook his head, turning to vault down the stone steps in the direction of the pool. He had made his decision, just as she had made hers. And by God he would live with it.

The night was surprisingly mild, with barely a breath of breeze blowing in from the bay. The moon was full and high in the sky, casting a silvery glow on the water of the pool.

He took no time in stripping down and diving in, shock coursing through him as the cold water encased his skin, penetrating through to his very core. The pool was deep and he pushed himself to his limit, waiting as long as possible before breaking the surface.

As the balmy air refilled his lungs he saw the unmistakable silhouette of Olivia, standing near the water's edge.

Roman stood, so that the water reached his waist, very aware that he was completely nude in the water. His heart beat slow and hard in his chest. They were silent for a long moment, his eyes never leaving hers.

'You decided to take a late-night swim,' she said, her voice strangely husky in the dim light.

'And you followed me.'

She moved to the entry steps of the pool, dipping one toe in before stepping down ankle-deep in the water.

He noticed for the first time that her legs and feet were bare, that she wore a thin robe that stopped just above her knee. He wondered if she had anything underneath. He felt an ache in his gut, so deep, and he knew right then that he would move heaven and earth to have her out of that robe and in his arms.

He moved forward in the water, closer to her with every breath.

'I decided I couldn't leave here tomorrow without knowing more about those fantasies,' she said, her voice carrying across the space between them loud and clear.

Her hands moved to the tie of her robe and Roman paused, feeling the breath freeze in his lungs as he simultaneously willed her to stop and to keep going.

'How much more?' he asked, his voice husky as it echoed off the pool walls.

'Everything,' she said, her eyes never leaving his.

Roman took another step and watched as Olivia's eyes dropped to where the water level now completely exposed him to her. Her eyes darkened as she looked, and looked, before finally dragging her gaze back up to meet his. What he saw there ignited a fire in his blood. Raw desire darkened her eyes and coloured her cheeks as she undid the tie of her robe.

The white silk slid from her skin and darkened as

it touched the water, leaving nothing between them but space. He was within arm's length of her now, unconsciously moving towards her. But he stilled at the sight of her, completely nude and offered to him like the living statue of a goddess. Her skin glowed under the moonlight. Every perfect curve of her body was on display in high definition and it was a revelation.

She stood still for a moment, before modesty got the better of her and she self-consciously moved one hand to shield her most intimate parts from his hungry gaze.

Roman closed the distance between them in a single movement, encircling her waist with his hands and pulling her with him into the water. With her body partially hidden, she relaxed in his arms and pressed herself tightly against him.

'I changed my mind too,' Roman said throatily, his mouth tracing a path along the exposed curve of her neck.

Her hands refused to stay clasped at his neck, instead preferring to explore the muscles of his back and down his waist.

She bit her lip seductively, removing her nails from where they had pinched quite roughly. 'I have wanted to do that for quite a while now.'

'Oh, so we are making up for lost time?' He gathered her higher, to his chest, wrapping one of her legs around his waist before doing the same with the

hurricane—being swept up into a power so much stronger than herself.

When she finally found her release Roman was right there to catch her and hold her as she fell back down to earth. Heat spread out across her body, sending electricity right down to the tips of her toes. She opened her eyes and realised she was being lifted out of the water as her skin came into contact with the cold lip of the pool.

The contact was brief, as Roman lifted himself out and gathered her up into his arms as though she weighed nothing at all. It was strange, allowing him to carry her naked across the terrace. They were completely alone on the island, so privacy was guaranteed, and as she looked up at him she realised the feeling she had was not one of nervousness but one of anticipation.

He carried her easily up the stairs to his master suite. She had barely taken in the cool grey sheets on the gigantic bed when she felt her anticipation quickly intensify to mild panic. He was advancing on her now, his perfect muscular torso glowing in the light of a single lamp as he lowered himself over her and cupped her face with one hand.

As his lips lowered to touch hers she turned her cheek, grimacing when she realised what she had done.

'Is everything okay?' he whispered from above her, one hand trailing down her shoulder in a slow, sensual path. 'Are you…rethinking this?'

'No,' she said quickly, noting his features soften with relief. 'No, I'm definitely not rethinking *any* of this.'

'Relax,' he murmured, kissing a path down between the valley of her breasts. 'This is one of those fantasies I was telling you about.'

'It is?'

She lay back, staring up at the ceiling and willing herself to calm down. His mouth was doing a very good job of distracting her. That was until she realised just where those lips were headed. She tensed, reaching down for him just as his lips began to trace a path below her navel.

'This is *my* fantasy, remember?' he said, gripping her wrists and holding them by her sides. 'And I haven't even got to the good part yet.'

'Roman...you can't honestly—'

'Do you trust me?' he asked, his eyes dark with passion as his lips pressed gentle kisses along the inside of her thigh.

Olivia watched him kiss her, watched him draw closer to the centre of her, and felt herself nod once. She did trust him. Completely.

The nerves fell away with each gentle kiss on her skin and her eyes never left him, watching as he drew his tongue slowly against the centre of her sex. Her back arched and her eyes fluttered closed for a moment. When she looked back down his eyes were on her, dark and possessive, as he moved his hands to spread her wide and kiss her even deeper.

Her head sank back against the pillows as her body was enveloped in wave after wave of hot, wet pleasure. She reached down and knitted her fingers through his hair, anchoring him to the spot that felt most intense. He growled his appreciation, sliding one finger inside her in a slow rhythm.

'Oh... Roman...' She gasped at the feeling of delicious fullness, hardly believing it when he added a second digit to join the first without breaking rhythm.

Just as she began to feel that pressure mounting once more he removed his mouth, sliding up her body in one fluid movement. He reached across to the nightstand, grabbing a small foil packet and sheathing himself with lightning speed.

'I can't wait another second. This time I want to be inside you when you come,' he rasped, his voice half demand, half question as he met her eyes in the dim glowing light.

She spread her legs wide, silently answering his question with her body.

She could feel the tension in his shoulders as he positioned himself at her entrance, slick and ready from his expert attentions. His breathing hitched as he entered her with exaggerated slowness. Olivia raised her legs to encircle his waist, showing him that she was ready. That she wanted to feel him inside her for the first time.

The feeling of fullness was so intense she almost begged him to stop. After a moment she wanted to ask if there was much more of him to go.

There was.

She breathed deep as the sensation became uncomfortable, and was vaguely aware of Roman's voice intruding on her thoughts.

'I'm hurting you,' he said, deeply concerned, and began to withdraw from her.

Olivia held him with her thighs, keeping them connected as her body adjusted to his sizeable girth. 'Now it's your turn to be patient,' she breathed.

She tested her hips once, then twice, in a slow rolling movement. What had begun as a dull sting of pressure soon gave way to a more pleasurable pulse of heat.

Roman's breath hissed from between his teeth as she moved against him, but he remained exaggeratedly still above her.

'Does that feel good for you?' Olivia asked, taking in his tense jaw and serious expression as she tightened her innermost muscles, feeling the delicious hardness of him buried inside her.

Roman lowered his face into the crook of her neck, groaning low in his throat as though he was in pain. 'Oh, yes. Oh, God, yes.'

Olivia smiled, moving against him and feeling his

breathing quicken in response. Suddenly he moved over her, his body arching slowly to press more firmly against her. She looked up into his eyes and somehow knew just what he needed.

He moved her thighs high on his waist, spreading her wide so that he could thrust right to the hilt. She gasped in pleasure, her hands on his chest as he braced himself on his forearms above her. His rhythm was deep and purposeful as he moved over her. He was powerful and entirely lost in his own pleasure.

Release reached them both at the same time, crashing down in wave after wave of pleasure. Olivia closed her eyes as the last of the ripples flowed through her, feeling the mattress move as Roman lay himself down heavily beside her.

CHAPTER NINE

ROMAN LAY STILL for a long time, his brain working overtime to fight through the heavy fog that always came after orgasm. This was different—heavier, somehow. He had never experienced a climax so intense.

Thoughts of why he should not feel so relaxed threatened the edges of his consciousness but he fought them off. He would analyse the repercussions of what they had just done in the morning, for now he thoroughly intended to repeat the experience just as soon as she was able.

He turned on his side, looking down at her where she lay curled on her side. Her eyes were closed, and for a moment he wondered if she was asleep, but then her lashes fluttered open and he was pinned by that blue-green gaze. Her hair had come undone at some stage, and its long lengths were spread across his sombre grey pillows in all their vibrant red glory. If possible, it looked even redder in that moment.

He reached out, taking a strand in his hands and running his fingers along the length of it. He was suddenly overcome by the realisation that it had been her first time and he had almost taken her in the swimming pool. Thankfully his brain hadn't been too far gone to realise that she deserved an actual bed for such a delicate moment, and that they needed to use protection. He *never* forgot to take precautions.

'I hope that was...satisfactory?' He smiled, a glow of male pride in his chest as he took in the slow smile that spread across her face.

'I never even dreamed that it could be so...' she began, shaking her head. 'Earth-shattering.'

'It isn't always that way.'

He ran a finger down the valley of her breasts, watching the play of light on her flawless skin. He had only just finished making love to her and he yet he couldn't stop touching her.

'I'm glad my first time was with you,' she said softly.

Roman stilled, taking in the look of deep emotion in her eyes. Knowing his own personal warning bells should be ringing at full blast. She was not experienced enough to separate the physical side of what they had just shared from her emotional reaction. And yet even as he told himself to remind her of his rules he found that he himself was having a hard time abiding by them.

He fought the urge to lean in, to kiss her mouth

and lay a trail of kisses down her neck. He frowned. Such actions were dangerously close to tenderness. He was not a tender lover—to a virgin or not.

But he cared what she thought of him, that she'd enjoyed her first time—that was entirely normal, wasn't it?

Maybe that was the problem. He had nothing to compare it to, having steered clear of virgins up to now. He had never enjoyed the idea of being a woman's first, of having that much pressure on the act. But now, knowing he was the only one to have touched her, been inside her, heard her scream out in her orgasm…

He wanted more.

It was a dangerous madness, feeling like this. He had always prided himself on remaining detached and aloof from the women he chose to spend time with. They knew he wasn't in it for commitment. They got what they needed and left his bed satisfied as a result.

Olivia sighed deeply and moved so that she lay against his side. Her hand stroked up the inside of his wrist to his elbow and he looked down to see her curiously tracing the thick black band of ink that encircled his forearm.

He didn't think of the tattoo often—it was usually covered up and out of sight. But every now and then he found himself looking at it, thinking of the man who'd branded him, of the *life* that had branded him. And yet he had never had it removed.

'It's a gang tattoo,' he offered, not knowing why he suddenly felt the urge to explain. 'Not my own personal choice of design.'

Her lips formed a delicate little O as her fingers stilled over him. 'From your time in prison?' she asked quietly.

'Long before prison.'

A silence fell between them. Roman wondered if perhaps she was regretting her choice of lover after his revelation, but after a moment she sat up on her elbow, pinning him with her gaze.

'This gang—did they use guns a lot? Is that where your fear stems from?'

Roman frowned, laying his head back against the pillows as he remembered the events of the day before in painful detail. 'No. That's not where it comes from.'

She seemed suddenly self-conscious. 'I'm sorry if this isn't exactly pillow-talk material. I know you are probably the kind of guy who doesn't like to talk afterwards.'

'I don't,' he said honestly. 'But I can compromise.' He turned smoothly onto his side, so that they were face to face. 'You can ask me *one* question about my past and I will answer it—truthfully.'

Her eyelashes lowered momentarily. 'Who is Sofiya?'

Roman was silent for a moment. Then, 'Sofiya was my little sister,' he said. 'She died a long time ago.'

'Oh, I'm sorry.' Olivia's brow deepened into a frown. 'She must have been very young.'

'Sixteen.' He shrugged. 'It's in the past. Almost twenty years ago.'

'Grief doesn't care about time.' The corners of her lips tilted down sadly. 'My grandmother was buried ten years ago and I still visit her grave often.'

'I have never visited Sofiya's resting place,' Roman said, surprised at how easily the words spilled from him. 'Her parents despised me.'

Olivia sat up slightly. '*Her* parents? Not yours?'

'We were both abandoned by our birth mother at a very young age. Sofiya was a tiny blonde cherub with big blue eyes. She was adopted very quickly. I was not.'

'Oh…' She sat up slightly, looking down at him with concern.

He hated the feeling of being so vulnerable, and yet somehow he was unable to stop the words from coming once they'd started. 'Unlike my sister, I wasn't the most appealing child. I always had too much to say. It became a part of me to cause as much trouble as I could manage.'

He frowned, remembering the uncontrollable rage that had filled him as a child. He had broken toys, furniture—even bones on a few occasions.

'I was fuelled by anger and hatred. I was kept at

the orphanage until I grew too big to contain. After I ran away for the third time they stopped trying to bring me back.'

'That is when you became homeless?'

Roman nodded. But the truth was he had never known a home. The only difference was that once he'd left the orphanage he'd had the added struggle of finding a safe place to sleep at night.

'I can't imagine how that was for a young boy.'

'I was thirteen—practically a man.' A low, harsh laugh escaped his lips as he thought of his gangly young self, so cocky and self-assured. 'When the local thugs saw the size of me they asked me to run errands. I didn't mind that they were criminals. They took me in...gave me a warm bed. One of the guys even bought me shoes.'

His chest tightened at the memory. He had worn those shoes until his feet had burst out of them. Then he had gone out and stolen himself a brand-new pair.

'I was thin and fast. They used me to climb through windows and vents and such on jobs. I felt very important.'

Olivia was quiet as he spoke on, telling her of his ascent into the criminal gangs of St Petersburg. To her credit, she did not react in any way other than to ask a question or to clarify a point. She just listened.

She listened when he told her of Alexi—the father of 'the brotherhood', as he'd called it. She nodded as he told her how, when he had grown broader and stronger, he had advanced to being a part of the main crew. They'd held up banks, intercepted cash in transit and generally just taken whatever they wanted. More than once he felt the old shame seep in, threatening to silence him, but she urged him on.

'This Alexi guy...he sounds dangerous,' she said softly, tracing a small circle on his chest as she watched him.

Roman thought for a moment of the man who had simultaneously given him everything and then torn his life to pieces.

'I wanted nothing more than for Alexi to be proud of me. He was the only dominant male figure I had ever known. It made me feel needed, validated—I don't know.' He shook his head, uncomfortable with the conversation all of a sudden. He didn't like to think of Alexi, of the hold he had once had on him.

'I think that was only natural. You were easily groomed—an easy target. You were vulnerable and he exploited that.'

'I never truly relaxed into the so-called brotherhood, and Alexi could see that. I had seen how quickly some of their drunken brawls escalated and I made a point to always stay sober. More than once he questioned my loyalty using violence.'

'Is *that* where your issue with guns stems from?' she asked quietly.

Roman frowned, realising he had gone off on a

tangent. How had he kept on speaking for this length of time? Usually talking of the brotherhood and its fearless leader was enough to send him into silence for days, but something about Olivia had kept him talking...opening up.

Unwelcome memories assaulted his brain. Memories of the last night he had seen Alexi. Of the blood and the outrage and that pair of terrified, lifeless, baby-blue eyes.

Suddenly he couldn't talk any more. He stood up, walking to the terrace doors to look out at the night beyond. He shivered, feeling a cold that was not actually in the air but inside him. Ingrained in him.

Olivia bit her bottom lip hard as Roman remained completely silent by the doors and then watched as he walked into the bathroom, shutting the door behind him with finality. She had pushed too hard—her curiosity had been too overbearing. He was likely already planning the best way to tell her to leave.

He had made it perfectly clear that he was a one-night-only, no-snuggling type of guy—and here she was, initiating a psychotherapy session.

She lay back, throwing one arm across her face in mortification. She had just made love with this physically gifted specimen of a man and still she kept digging deeper, wanting more from him than he had warned her to expect. Trying to peek under his armour.

She angrily swung her legs over the side of the bed and stood, feeling her inner muscles throb with just the barest hint of exertion. She didn't feel too different, she thought with a frown. A little sore, perhaps, but not monumentally transformed as she had expected.

Still, it had been...utterly perfect.

Maybe it was best that it ended this way. She would arrange to have a helicopter pick her up in the morning and that would be it. No awkward morning-after encounter, no hurt feelings. They both knew what this was, that it could be nothing more. She was completely fine with that.

But still some small naïve part of her made her linger for a moment outside the bathroom door until she heard the shower turned on. He couldn't have sent a clearer signal if he'd shouted the words *Go away!* at the top of his lungs.

The night was over.

She returned to her bedroom in darkness, not bothering to turn on any lights as she slipped in between the cool white covers and let stillness wash over her. Her mind raced, thoughts of what tomorrow might bring seeping through to her consciousness as the afterglow of her one experience of lovemaking dimmed.

Was one night of perfect lovemaking with a man of her choosing really enough to carry her through a lifetime of a loveless marriage?

As her exhausted brain admitted defeat and she drifted into half-sleep, she imagined what her wedding day might look like. Only in her mind the man at the top of the aisle was Roman. Devastating in a dark tuxedo as he took her hand and professed his eternal love for her.

All of a sudden her dream shifted to their wedding night, becoming infinitely more erotic. She sighed as he leaned in and pressed his lips to hers, the scent of him so familiar and overwhelming it was as if she could actually feel the heat of his skin pressing against her.

'You are so beautiful...'

His voice rasped near her ear, sending shivers down her spine and even lower.

Her eyes snapped open. 'Roman?'

He was draped across her, the scent of his shower fresh and warm on the air as his mouth laid a trail of kisses down the side of her neck.

'You left without giving me a chance to say goodbye,' he said, a dark glint in his eye as he moved lower to take one of her breasts into his mouth.

'You were the one who left.' She exhaled on a slow hiss as his teeth grazed her skin. 'I thought you were a one-night-only kind of guy.'

A wicked smile spread over his dark features as he poised himself over her, one hand snaking a path down her abdomen to slip between her thighs.

'The night isn't over yet, Princess.'

His kisses became more heated as his fingers took her higher and higher towards climax. Before she could completely shatter, he turned onto his back and urged her to straddle him.

'You will still be tender... I don't want to hurt you,' he rasped, his breath coming hard and fast, evidence of his arousal.

Olivia moved over him so that her breasts grazed the smattering of dark hair on his chest. She was clumsy at first, uncertain in her own movements as she poised her body over the sizeable length of him. He was rock-hard and already sheathed, waiting for her. She took a moment to slide the tip of him against her most sensitive spot, enjoying the sensation of molten heat that spread through her.

She repeated the motion a few times, wondering if he would grow impatient and take over himself. He didn't. Even as his rigid jaw showed the extent of his control he remained still, allowing her this moment of exploration.

'I'm not quite sure if I'll be any good at this,' she said uncertainly, lifting herself so that he was poised at her entrance.

'I'm right here, holding you.' He ran his large hands down her back, cupping her buttocks with possession as he guided her.

Her body stretched around him as she took him deep inside her in one smooth movement. The barest hint of discomfort faded quickly to an impatient need to roll her hips, to ride him and increase the delicious pressure she could feel with each movement.

'Is that…good?' she asked, her breath coming faster as arousal pooled and tightened inside her.

'You are driving me insane in the best possible way,' he groaned, his eyes never leaving hers. 'Don't come yet. Not until I'm right there with you.'

Olivia tried to slow down, to control her movements and somehow hold off the mounting climax that seemed ready to shatter her entire being at any second. He held her gaze, his hands gripping her hips as he began thrusting upwards slowly, in time with her.

Their rhythm was so smooth, so gentle, and yet somehow it was filled with a barely restrained madness as they both rose closer and closer to climax. Roman's breath fanned hard and fast against her cheek as she leaned forward, her breasts crushed against his chest. His hands moved up her back to hold her close, a deep primal groan escaping his lips as he slowed down even further and moved deeper inside her.

Olivia gasped at the overwhelming intensity of being so absolutely cocooned in his strength, and then the intense friction tipped her over the edge and she fell headlong into an orgasm that seemed to ripple through every inch of her body.

As she fell she felt a tightening in her throat, and

prayed he wouldn't see the sheen of moisture in her eyes as she watched him lose control entirely beneath her.

Roman kissed her neck, growling something deeply erotic in his native tongue as the muscles of his abdomen began to ripple with the force of his own orgasm.

Afterwards, as she listened to his breathing deepen with sleep, she wondered if she had ever felt closer to another human being in her entire life.

The thought made her feel sad and grateful all at once. She had got her wish, without a doubt. He had made her first time the most sensual, real experience of her life.

His long, hard body was partly covered, but she still let her gaze sweep over him in the darkness, lingering on his features. His face was transformed in sleep, the hard lines of his mouth completely relaxed. It made him seem younger…more carefree. It dawned on her that she had never seen him look at peace. Here, in sleep, Roman the great and powerful master of security, was completely vulnerable.

The thought of returning to the palace, to her own empty bed, was suddenly inconceivable. And even worse was the thought of sleeping alongside another man.

Marrying another man.

Her throat tightened painfully with the force of her emotion. Roman would not offer her any more than this night—she knew that. He was not the mar-

rying kind, no matter what she suddenly hoped. He
was not even the relationship kind.

But as she lay staring up at the play of shadows
on the ceiling she knew one thing with more cer-
tainty than she had ever known anything in her life.

She would not marry the Sheikh.

When she awoke the bed was empty beside her in
the early-morning light. Ignoring the sting of loss,
she grabbed a white robe and stepped out onto the
terrace, taking a moment simply to breathe and take
in the gorgeous view of the bay spread out below.

Her hair was a nest of tangles, and she was in
dire need of a shower, but for once she had no formal breakfast to attend, no official functions. She
could stand here all morning if she chose, enjoying
the last few hours of her freedom.

Roman would expect her to leave today, and that
was perfectly understandable.

She thought of his revelations last night, the deep,
dark secrets he'd shared, and wondered if he would
regret sharing so much now that their night together
was done.

He had told her only briefly of his life in St Petersburg. Of the orphan who had been abandoned
to sleep in cold gutters, but she remembered every
word in vivid detail. Every little piece of the puzzle
he had revealed that made him what he was.

Roman had lived through hell itself. It was no

wonder he seemed harsh. The world had hardened him from the moment he was born. He shouldn't have had a chance—and yet he had risen from his old life, determined and hungry for better. He had created his own empire without a single care for his social class or his chequered past.

He was the master of his own destiny.

Here, in the rosy glow of dawn, she felt utterly transformed simply by having known him. She laughed at her own thoughts. Romantic, indeed, or maybe simply foolish. Perhaps all virgins felt this way about their first lover?

How would he react to the news once he found out that her marriage was not going ahead? She imagined he would be frustrated with her—with himself. He would blame it all on their brief affair.

But, truly, Olivia wasn't sure her decision was completely down to their night together. On some level she had known she was not destined for a love-less marriage from the moment her father had thrust the idea upon her.

No amount of loyalty to Monteverre would out-weigh the value she needed to feel in herself. Roman had made her see that, somehow.

She told herself that it didn't bother her that he was completely unaffected by their time together. She was not going to read anything into last night, and nor would she expect anything more from their liaison. He had made it very clear that he was not the kind of guy who slept with the same woman twice.

CHAPTER TEN

ROMAN HAD TOLD Jorge to take the day off, to ensure them some privacy, wanting as little intrusion as possible so that he could deal with the aftermath of their night together.

Olivia arrived down to breakfast dressed in pink. The dress had the kind of high waist and flowing, knee-length bell-shaped skirt that made her appear like something straight from a vintage movie.

She was breathtaking.

Her eyes were shuttered and her smile forced as she sat at the table across from him. The silence was heavy and uncomfortable, and his mind scrambled to find something to break the tension. In the end he accepted that there was simply nothing to say.

To his amazement, Olivia demolished two full plates of fresh fruit and a cream-drizzled pastry. She moaned as she devoured her last bite of pastry, looking up to find his eyes trained on her.

'I was hungry,' she said, a light blush on her cheeks.

'I've seen prison inmates eat with more decorum,' he found himself saying playfully. 'One night with me and you've completely forgotten how to behave like a princess.'

Her eyes widened at his mention of last night, as though he had broken some unwritten rule by acknowledging that it had happened.

She sat back in her seat, a smile crossing her lips as she met his eyes boldly. 'Whatever will my subjects think?'

Roman raised a brow. 'That you've been taken down the path to ruin by a disreputable mongrel.'

'Mongrel?' She looked both amused and shocked.

'You come from a world where breeding is everything, after all.'

'Have we suddenly become *Lady and the Tramp*?' She laughed.

'I have no idea what that is,' he said honestly, smiling at the look of horrified surprise on her face.

'I can't believe you've never seen such a classic. It's wonderful—the lady dog comes from a fancy home and gets lost, and the tramp dog saves her?'

'You are likening me to a tramp dog?' He raised one brow in disbelief. 'I'm flattered.'

'*You* likened yourself to a mongrel—not me!' she exclaimed. 'It's not *my* fault that my brain associates everything with movies.'

'Film and television were not a regular part of my childhood,' he said, disliking where this conversation was headed. 'But let me guess: they all live happily ever after at the end?'

'Yes, exactly.' She smiled.

'That's why I don't waste my time on movies. It's not reality.'

'Well, of *course* it's not reality.' She laughed. 'That's what makes them an escape.'

Roman stood, gathering their plates and placing them less than gently into the sink. 'You spend far too much of your time escaping real life—you know that?' he said, knowing he had hit a nerve when he looked up and saw both of her hands balled into fists on the tabletop.

'You're being cruel now, and I have no idea why.'

'This is not cruelty, Olivia,' he said calmly. 'You have no idea what true cruelty is. What true hardship is, even. You dislike it when people put real life in front of you—that's your problem.'

She shook her head slowly. 'I have no idea why you're being like this right now. We were just talking about a movie.'

'Life is not like the movies, and the sooner you realise it the better!' He raised his voice, surprising himself with the force of his outburst.

Olivia stood, closing the distance between them. 'I may not have known the kind of hardship that you have experienced in your life, but that does not negate the fact that I have feelings too.'

'I thought it was clear that last night was not about feelings,' he said stiffly.

'And yet here you stand, shouting at me, when I was perfectly prepared to leave here on good terms.' She shook her head. 'It's probably best that I wait outside until my helicopter arrives.'

'You are leaving?' he said, the words tasting like sawdust in his mouth.

'I called the palace first thing this morning. They are sending someone to get me.' She nodded, moving to the table to pick up her coffee cup before returning to place it in the sink.

Even with her perfect posture and impeccably coiffed hair she seemed quite at ease, clearing up after herself. Far from a domesticated goddess, but still not too far above herself to consider leaving the mess for him to clean.

He thought of their conversations the evening before, of her talk of charity work. She was not the pampered royal he'd accused her of being and it was high time he admitted it to himself.

It was easy to place her in that box—to see her as stuck up and untouchable. It made her less real. But here she was, the woman who had shattered something inside him with her lovemaking last night, all too real.

And all too ready to leave him.

He knew then why he was being cruel. He simply wasn't ready to give this up. To give *her* up. Not yet. And yet he knew it had already gone on too long as it was.

He was the worst kind of bastard, he thought darkly. Khal had trusted him with this—had entrusted him with the care of the woman he hoped to spend the rest of his life with. Whether the union was cold and political or not, it did not matter. He had rationalised his actions simply because their passion had been mutual. He had got lost in the novelty of feeling so utterly out of control.

Olivia deserved more than this. She deserved more than a brief fling with a man like him. And that was all he could offer her. Once the passion wore off he would only end up hurting her when he left. Roman Lazarov did not *do* relationships. He did not make declarations of love and commitment or plan lifetimes together.

In the past he had never been good at returning the things he had stolen. He refused to repeat his mistakes. And yet the idea of Khal knowing what had happened made him balk. Not for himself, but for Olivia. She deserved his protection.

'I'm coming with you,' he said, surprising himself.

Olivia turned around, her eyes wide with confusion. 'There is no need to escort me home, noble as it seems.'

'This is not about being noble—it's about being honest with Khal.'

Guilt entered her expression at the mention of the Sheikh's name. His gut churned at the realisation that by rights he should be displaying the same emotions himself, seeing as he had spent the past twelve hours in bed with the woman his best friend hoped to marry.

'Do you honestly want us to tell him about last night?' she said with disbelief.

'I will speak to him alone. There is no need for you to see him.' He found himself saying the words—words he had meant to protect her—and yet he could tell by the dark look on her face that they had come out wrong. As usual.

'You presume that I need you to explain on my behalf.' Her gaze seemed to darken as he took a step closer to her. She stood tall. 'I am quite capable of speaking for myself.'

'Clearly you are not. Otherwise none of this would have happened.' Roman shook his head, anger at the whole ridiculous situation coursing through him.

'Feeling some remorse, I see.' She pursed her lips.

'*One* of us should. Do you simply plan to go back and accept his proposal with the heat from my bed barely gone from your skin?'

'Is that actually what you think of me? Do you even know me at *all*?' She was completely still, unnaturally still, like the eerily calm glass of the ocean before a hurricane.

'I'm trying to—God help me. But you're not making it very easy.'

'And just what will you tell him? Seeing as you've got this covered.'

'Whatever needs to be said. Bottom line: he needs to know that we have slept together. I cannot let your marriage go ahead with him in the dark.'

'Bottom line?' Olivia's eyes widened. 'You know that telling him will essentially be ending the engagement before it can even happen? Why the sudden change of heart? Two days ago you were doing everything in your power to make this union go ahead.'

'Do I truly need to explain to you what has changed?'

Olivia's eyes darkened. 'Yes. You do.'

And there it was. The gauntlet, large and heavy, hanging in the tension-charged air between them.

'You spent the night with me, Olivia,' he said. 'I took your virginity.'

'That does not qualify as an explanation.' She bit one side of her lip, taking a few paces away from him before turning back. 'You said it yourself—it was just sex.'

Roman met the unmistakable challenge in her blue-green eyes. He had not lied when he'd told her that sex was not always so intense.

'Sex is never "just sex" when it is one person's first time,' he said quietly, knowing he was being a complete coward.

'I think that is up to me to decide.'

'You wouldn't need to decide anything if I had done the right thing and walked away last night.'

'How utterly male of you to think that.' She rolled her eyes. 'Spending the night in your bed was *my* choice too, Roman. I wanted it just as much. I wanted *you*.' Olivia took a step towards him, the sunlight glowing on her Titian waves. 'You did not *take* my virginity. You can't take something that is given freely. I took last night just as much as you did.'

She looked so beautiful at that moment—all strength and feminine power. Hadn't he told her she needed to let this woman be free?

The unmistakable sound of helicopter blades in the distance intruded on the moment. Roman looked out of the windows and sure enough a scarlet-coloured chopper was coming in from the coast, the gold crest of Monteverre emblazoned along its side.

I wanted you.

Her words echoed in his mind as he analysed his own motivation for wanting to tell Khal of their night together. He knew that telling his friend would stop the engagement, knowing Khal as he did. He still wanted her. He was not fool enough to deny the fact. One night was just not enough when it came to Olivia. She was the best and the worst thing that he had ever stolen in his life, and the bastard in him wanted to keep her here until they were both truly done with each other.

Was he really that selfish? To manipulate her situation and push Khal out of the picture simply so that he could get her out of his system?

He ran one hand through the short crop of his hair, trying to make sense of his own thoughts.

'What if I told you that I plan to refuse the marriage?'

Her voice was quiet from behind him, strangely uncertain after the power of her speech moments before.

'You said yourself that your loyalty to your country is important.'

'Yes, but that was before I realised how it felt to take control of my own life for once.' She bit her bottom lip. 'Being with you…it's made me realise that I can have more. That I want more.'

'I can't give you what you want,' he said plainly, panicking at the look of open emotion on her face. 'If you plan on placing your entire future on the hope of something more between us then you are more naïve than I originally thought.'

She flinched at his harsh words and he felt like the worst kind of bastard. Hearing her speak of their time together so tenderly did strange things to his chest. As if with every word she uttered, bands grew tighter around his lungs. And it made him want to lash out with words to make her stop. To make her see him for what he was.

It was ridiculous, and immature, and yet he could

no more stop himself from reacting that way than he could stop his brain from seeing guns where they didn't exist.

Olivia fought the tightness in her throat, refusing to let him see how deeply his words had cut. She met his gaze evenly. 'I will be returning to the palace alone. I trust that you will respect my privacy when it comes to last night. I should at least have the right to that from you.'

'I never said I didn't respect you,' he said harshly.

'Good. We have an understanding.'

She kept her voice even, walking over to the terrace doors to watch as the helicopter finished its landing and a familiar assistant exited the door, making her way towards the villa.

'This is goodbye, then,' she said, not wanting to turn to look at him but knowing she would regret it for ever if she didn't. She felt anger, hot and heavy, burning in her chest. 'Thank you for allowing me to be one of the many women in your bed.'

His eyes narrowed, a cynical snarl appearing on his lips. 'Indeed. I will always have the pleasure of knowing that when it comes to you I was the first.'

'You are using the past tense already—how honest of you.'

'I have been nothing but honest with you about the kind of man I am,' he said harshly.

'Last night…I just thought that things seemed

different somehow. That *we* seemed different.' She spoke calmly, trying and failing to hide the hint of insecurity in her voice.

'Everything seems different in the heat of passion, Printsessa.'

The silence that followed might only have lasted a matter of seconds, but to Olivia it felt like an eternity. In her mind she willed him to say more. Even a hint that he felt something more would be enough. Had she truly imagined that last night was momentous for them both?

And then he turned from her. Every step that he took across the kitchen seemed to hammer into her heart. Dampening down any flicker of hope she might have had.

She listened as his footsteps echoed across the marble tiles. Did he pause for just a split second in the doorway or did she imagine it? For a moment she thought he had taken a breath, preparing to speak. But then his steps kept going, out into the hallway, echoing as he moved further and further away from her.

She let out a breath that she hadn't even realised she'd been holding. The air shuddered through a gap in her teeth, like a balloon deflating and making a spectacular nosedive towards the ground. It was the ultimate heartbreak…knowing she had been just another woman in his bed.

She wanted to be *the* woman. The *only* woman.

But hadn't he made it abundantly clear that he would never be that kind of man? Was she really such a clichéd, naïve little virgin that she had fallen head over heels in love with him and expected him to do the same?

Typical that there wasn't a drop of vodka on the damned boat when he needed it.

Roman threw the empty bottle down hard on the glass bar-top, feeling it crack and shatter in his hand as it hit the surface.

'*Chert voz'mi!*'

He held his hand over the sink as the first drops of blood began to fall. The cuts were not deep, just surface wounds.

'*Damn* whoever is in charge of stocking the damned bar.'

'That would be me, sir.'

Roman turned to see Jorge in the open doorway, the man's face filled with concern.

'I came to see if you want me to close up the house.'

'Do whatever you like. I won't staying around long enough to check.'

'I see that Olivia has left us,' Jorge said tentatively.

Roman lowered his voice. 'I do not want to speak about Olivia. I want to relax and enjoy the rest of my vacation on my damned boat—alone.'

'With vodka?' Jorge added.

'Yes. With vodka. Is there a problem with that?' Roman spat. 'I am a grown man and you are not my father.'

'No. No, I am not,' Jorge said, a hint of sadness in his voice. 'But you have made it clear in the past that you at least see me as a friend of sorts.'

Roman grunted, wrapping a strip of linen carelessly around his injured hand.

'Can I speak frankly with you?' Jorge asked.

'You always do.'

The older man half smiled, crossing his arms and taking a deep breath before speaking. 'I think that you are hurting right now.'

'Believe me, I've had worse in my lifetime. I'll heal.'

'I'm not talking about the cuts on your hands.'

'Neither am I.'

'The Roman I know would never concede defeat so easily. You are not the kind of stupid man who would let pride stand in the way of what he wants.'

'Just because I want something, it doesn't mean I should have it. I have learnt that lesson in the past, Jorge. She is meant for a better man than me. A *good* man.'

'She loves you.'

'No. She is in love with the *idea* of love and nothing more.'

'I watched her get into that helicopter and, believe me, I know a heartbroken woman when I see one.'

'Well, that's not my fault. I did not hide from her the man that I am.'

'The man that you are would never come railing into his liquor cabinet unless he was deeply hurt by something. Or someone.'

'Jorge, you really must add psychoanalysis to your list of skills.'

'Tell me I'm wrong,' the other man said. 'Tell me she doesn't mean anything to you and I will fill that bar with vodka and send you on your way.'

'She is nothing to me,' he said the words, willing himself to believe them. Willing himself to ignore the burning pit of anger in his stomach.

'So if Khal marries her you will stand by his side and wish them well? I can see it now. You can visit them each summer in Zayyar. If you are lucky, their children might even call you Uncle.'

Roman's eyes snapped up to meet the gaze of his all too knowing housekeeper.

'*There.* That's all the reaction I needed to see.'

'Just because I feel the marriage is the wrong choice for both of them, it doesn't mean there is something deeper going on. I know Khal, and I know he would not be happy with a woman like Olivia. She is too adventurous, too unpredictable. She wants to see the world, to be surprised by life. Not trade one palace prison for another.'

'And have you said any of this to the woman herself?'

Roman sat down on the bar stool, pulling the linen tighter on his hand and feeling the sting of pain that came with it. Jorge was right. He had not told Olivia how he felt about the marriage. Not honestly. He had spent half his time with her trying to convince her to marry Khal, and the other half trying to make her forget.

Was it really surprising that she had run from him again at the first chance? From the start he had handled her badly.

Women like Olivia were out of his league. She was too open, too caring and kind-hearted for a cold, unfeeling bastard like him. She deserved love. She deserved the happy-ever-after that she craved. And if he couldn't give it to her himself then he would make damned sure that she had a decent chance of finding it elsewhere.

'Shall I have the boat readied for departure?' Jorge asked hopefully.

Roman nodded once, watching as his housekeeper practically skipped from the room. He really should give that man a raise, he thought darkly as he moved to look out at the waves crashing against the light-house in the distance.

The marriage would not go ahead—not if he had anything to do with it.

CHAPTER ELEVEN

THE FIRST THING that Roman noticed as he entered the Sheikh's penthouse hotel suite was the utter stillness of the place. A single palace guard welcomed him inside before returning to his post outside the doorway. There was no butler to accept his coat or announce his presence—in fact no one at all roamed the halls as he passed through from room to room.

He had almost given up when finally he reached a large dining room that looked out over the lush green mountainscape of Monteverre's famous rolling hills. Khal stood alone at the head of the long dining table, his back turned as he stared out at the view.

Roman cleared his throat, feeling as though he had interrupted a moment of quiet meditation and wishing he had called ahead of his arrival.

'Roman. Now, this *is* a surprise,' Khal said, surprise filtering into his dark features as recognition dawned.

But Roman had not missed the mask of dark stillness that had been on his friend's face. That look bothered him deeply, and yet he knew that if he asked his concern would be met with a stone wall.

They were much alike, he and Khal.

'I need to speak with you,' Roman started, finding the words much more difficult than he had anticipated.

Truthfully, he was unsure where to begin. He had come here, all guns blazing, ready to rock the boat and make sure this ridiculous marriage did not go ahead. But how exactly did he tell his best friend that he had not only broken a rather important promise, but that he had done it in the worst way possible? He had promised to bring the Princess back to Monteverre to take her place as Khal's future wife, and instead...

Well, instead he had found himself consumed by a passion and a need so intense it had bordered on obsession.

He had not stopped thinking of Olivia in the few hours they had been apart. Memories of her assaulted him at every turn. If he closed his eyes he could almost smell the warm vanilla scent of her hair as it had lain spread across his pillows. He could almost hear her throaty laughter. She consumed him like no other woman ever had.

In fact, it was a mark of the strength of his feelings for her that he chose *not* to fight for her.

He was not here to lay claim to her.

He was here to set her free.

Khal sat heavily in one of the high-backed chairs, putting his feet up on the marble tabletop and surveying Roman with one raised brow. 'By all means, speak.'

'The Princess is the wrong choice for your bride.' He met Khal's gaze purposefully, making sure that there was no mistaking the seriousness of his tone.

'You sound quite sure.'

'I am. And I would like you to take my concern into account. There are things more important in life than politics.'

'Such as friendship, perhaps?' the Sheikh suggested, a strange hint of cynicism in his voice.

'I was thinking more along the lines of personal happiness.'

'I'm touched, Roman. Truly.'

'I'm trying to do the right thing here. To stop you from making a mistake that will last the rest of your life.'

'If you were doing the right thing you would be telling me the truth. You see, you need not worry about my personal happiness at all, Lazarov. Princess Olivia has already made her refusal of marriage to me quite clear.'

Roman felt his chest tighten painfully. 'Olivia? She came to you?'

'Not long before you, actually. Strangely, when she spoke of you she bore the same look on her face as you do right now when I mention her name.'

Hot guilt burned low in his stomach as his friend stood up and met his eyes with a cold detached evenness he had never witnessed before.

'I'm trying to control my temper here, Roman, because I don't want to jump to conclusions. But I'm struggling. Three months of planning. The future of two kingdoms hanging in the balance. And after a few days with you she's ready to give everything up.'

Roman remained silent for a moment, taking in the glint of barely controlled temper visible in his oldest friend's eyes. He knew he should walk away before things became any more heated. Olivia had already refused the marriage—he had no reason to be here.

But something held him rooted to the spot. In his mind all he could picture was King Fabian, planning Olivia's life for months before informing her of her impending engagement. Using an innocent woman as a pawn in his own political games. The man was cold enough to practically sell his own daughter to the highest bidder—as though she were a commodity rather than his own flesh and blood. It made the proud, possessive street thug inside him roar to life and demand justice.

'Tell me something,' he said calmly. 'In your three months of planning did you ever think to speak to the woman herself to see if she *wanted* a political marriage?'

He watched Khal's mouth harden into a tight line

as they stood toe to toe in the utterly silent dining room. There were no onlookers here, no palace guards or servants. They did not need to maintain any level of propriety. Right now they were just two men.

'I will ask *you* this question, because I deemed it inappropriate to ask the lady herself.' Khal's voice was a low whisper. 'Did you sleep with her, Roman?'

'Yes. I did,' Roman said the words harshly, feeling the air crackle with tension between them. 'And I am not going to apologise. Not to you, or to her damned father, or anybody.'

'Well, I'm glad to see you showing some remorse.'

'She is a *person*, Khal,' Roman spat. 'Not mine or yours. She can make her own damned choices— which you would know if you had ever bothered to treat her as such.'

'Right now this has nothing to do with her and *everything* to do with you,' Khal snarled, taking a step forward and jamming one finger hard against Roman's shoulder. 'You just couldn't control yourself—admit it. You wanted a woman and so you had her. Does the Princess *know* that she is just another notch on your bedpost? Or perhaps you are both just as selfish and impulsive as each other?'

Roman surged forward. Their noses were now mere inches apart. 'She is *nothing* like me,' he said coldly. 'She is kind and giving and she deserves more in a man than either of us could ever offer her.'

He paused, watching the anger drain from Khal's

face as his brows furrowed with surprise. With a deep, shuddering breath he stepped away, turning to face the window.

A long moment of deathly silence passed before he heard Khal exhale slow and hard behind him, a slight whistle escaping his lips. 'I don't believe this... You are in love with her.'

Roman braced one hand on the window ledge, looking out and seeing nothing. 'Don't be a fool. You said it yourself—women have only ever served one purpose for me.'

Khal's low whistle of laughter sounded across the room. 'I never thought I'd see this day. Roman Lazarov—brought to the edge of his infamous personal control by love.'

Roman shook his head, turning to take in the look of amused wonderment on the Sheikh's dark features. 'I am not prone to the sentiment. I simply believe Olivia has been treated poorly and I want to see it made right.'

'You poor, naïve fool. Sadly, love is not something we can choose to feel or not to feel. Trust me—I know.'

'I am not like you, Khal. I am not made for family life.' He took a deep breath, knowing it was finally time to say out loud the words that he had wanted to say for a long time. 'Look at my history with protecting the women I care for. My sister, your wife...

I break things. I always have. I am simply not the kind of man she needs me to be.'

The mention of his late wife was usually enough to put an end to any conversation, but Khal surprised him, standing and placing a hand heavily on his shoulder.

'It was not your fault that Priya was killed. I have told you this time and time again. Just as it was not your fault that Sofiya was killed. You cannot take on the blame for everything that goes wrong around you.'

'What about Zayyar?' Roman said, shaking his head. 'This marriage was part of your great plan and now it's all gone to crap.'

'Perhaps not,' Khal said cryptically. 'I am not completely out of options just yet. Once Olivia ran away, the King and I discussed a possible fallback plan.'

Roman was silent for a moment. 'The youngest Princess?'

Khal shrugged. 'If she is willing, so be it. If not, I will retreat and regroup—as always.'

Roman nodded, glad that all hope was not lost for the two nations.

Olivia stood in her dressing room and placed the elegant emerald tiara upon her head for the last time. She met her own eyes in the mirror with a mixture of sadness and excitement, knowing that after tonight everything would change.

And yet everything had already changed for her.

Would anyone notice that everything inside her had undergone a massive transformation in the past few days?

With sudden momentous clarity she realised that for the first time in her life she truly didn't care. From tomorrow she would be giving up her right to succeed to the throne voluntarily, and making the leap into actually leading Mimi's Foundation. She was done with being a pretty face who smiled and waved. The time had come for her to use her own two hands to make the difference she craved.

Perhaps once all of this was over she might appreciate this moment more—the sudden power she felt as she left her suite and began to descend the grand staircase on the way to take her life back into her own hands. But at that moment she felt neither powerful nor relieved.

She had given her virginity and her heart to a man who had repeatedly warned her that he would treasure neither. She knew now that romantic souls could not simply choose to behave otherwise. She could not switch off the part of herself that yearned to feel loved, no matter how much she willed herself to.

A lifetime of training had taught her how to relax her facial muscles into a polite mask of indifference, even while emotions threatened her composure. Harsh decisions would likely need to be made, and comfort zones abandoned. But for the first time in her twenty-six years she was not worried about the unknown.

Olivia couldn't recall the grand palace ballroom ever looking more beautiful. As she descended the long staircase into the crowd of guests below she reminded herself to smile and hold herself tall and proud.

Perhaps one day in the far future she might look back on this night and yearn for a moment like this. But even as the tug of uncertainty threatened she pushed it away. She had made her decision and the time had come to put herself first.

The Sheikh had not been half as forbidding as she had anticipated—in fact he had seemed more pensive than anything as she had carefully outlined her reasons for refusing his proposal. His gaze had seemed knowing as he had enquired about Roman's treatment of her, but perhaps that was just her own sense of guilt.

She had her own reasons for keeping her affair with Roman private. She wanted to treasure her time with him, not have it sullied by the judgement of others. Either way, she had taken her power back and it felt great. The marriage would not be going ahead.

But she was not naïve enough to think that the hardest part was over.

Even as the thought crossed her mind she looked up to see her father watching her from across the ballroom. They had not yet formally met, but by now she assumed he would have spoken with the Sheikh. He would know that she had refused the proposal and he would be planning his punishment for her supposed betrayal.

Let him plan, she thought with a solemn shake of her head. He had no control over her. Not any more.

A commotion near the entrance caught her eye and she looked up to the top of the staircase to see a man pushing past the guards to descend the steps with ease. Two Royal Zayyari guards in crisp white and purple uniforms flanked him, holding off the Monteverre palace guards with ease and forcing them to stand down.

Roman.

Her mind went completely blank as the man she loved advanced towards her, his powerful frame accentuated by a perfectly tailored tuxedo.

'What are you doing here?' she blurted, so taken off balance by his appearance that it made her insides shake.

'It's good to see you too, *milaya moya.*'

His voice was like a balm to her soul. She hadn't realised how much her silly lovesick heart had yearned to hear it again. Just one more time. It had barely been twenty-four hours since she had left Isla Arista, and yet it felt like a lifetime since she had stood in front of him. Since she had looked into his slate-grey eyes as he had broken her heart with all the practice of a pro.

He opened his mouth to speak, but was cut off by the booming voice of her father as he advanced upon them from the other side of the room.

'Guards! Get this criminal out of my palace this instant!' King Fabian was livid, his cheeks a bright puce as he came to a stop a few steps away from where Roman stood.

The ballroom seemed to have become very quiet all of a sudden, and Olivia was thankful that the room was only half full as the guests had only just started to arrive.

'King Fabian—I was hoping I would see you tonight.' Roman's eyes narrowed, his shoulders straightening with sudden purpose.

Olivia reached out as Roman took a step towards her father, her hand on his arm stilling his movements. 'This is my fight, not yours,' she said, steeling herself as she turned to her father.

'The Sheikh has said that you refused his proposal after your little trip with this thug,' King Fabian spat. 'Judging by the lovesick puppy expression on his face, I can take a good guess as to why.'

Roman snarled, but remained dutifully silent.

'Father, I had planned to have this conversation at a better time,' she said, looking around to see that the palace guards had descended to herd the guests to the other side of the room, offering the royal family some privacy.

'There is nothing you can say to save yourself

now, girl.' Her father shook his head sadly. 'I hope he's worth giving up your place in this family.'

'He has nothing to do with me giving up my place,' she said, as Roman frowned. 'Well, he does— but not in the way that you think.'

She took a deep breath, facing her father head-on.

'By giving up my right to succeed to the throne I am free of your control. That's worth more to me than being a princess ever could be.'

Roman reached out to touch her arm, 'Olivia, you don't have to do this.'

'I do. You see, my father has made more life-altering decisions on my behalf than this one.' She looked back at her father, noting his gaze darken. 'Such as when I inherited sole ownership of my grandmother's foundation ten years ago and he had me sign away my rights to him. At sixteen years old I didn't understand the repercussions. But now I do. And I know that by stepping out from under your thumb I'll get to take control of my own destiny for once and truly start helping people.'

'You can't do that.' King Fabian laughed cruelly. 'You can't simply walk away from this life.'

'I already have, Father,' she said sadly. 'I've been in contact with external advisors over the past few months to discuss the legalities. Once I relinquish any claim I have to the throne the foundation goes back into my name alone. Just as Mimi wished it to be.'

She hated it that her own father could look at her with such open disgust simply because she had chosen to go against his wishes.

Her own personal happiness did not matter to him.

Roman's eyes had widened as he listened to the exchange but he did not speak for her again. Nor did he attempt to interrupt as Olivia finished her conversation with her father and simply turned and walked away.

He took a moment to stand toe to toe with His Majesty, King Fabian. The urge to say everything he wished to say was so intense it consumed him. But Olivia had handled the situation with all the style and grace of the Princess she truly was. There was nothing he could add that wouldn't ruin it.

And so he walked away, following the woman he loved and ignoring the slew of vulgar curses in Catalan shouted in his wake.

He followed her in the direction of the outer terrace, instructing the two Zayyari guards Khal had lent him to stand sentry by the doors and make sure they were undisturbed.

Olivia stood with her back to him, staring out at where the moonlight shone across the ornamental pond in the gardens.

He moved to her side, reaching out his hand, needing to touch her. She flinched away and something inside him flinched too, with the hurt of that small movement.

'You're angry with me…of course you are,' he said softly, silently urging her to turn to look at him.

She didn't speak. Instead she wrapped her arms around herself defensively and stared resolutely ahead.

'I came here because I wanted to save you,' he said. 'I never even entertained the possibility that you were completely capable of saving yourself.'

'I'm glad I surprised you,' she said, irony dripping from her words as she turned to face him.

'Olivia…' he breathed. 'I came here to make sure that the marriage would not go ahead. I told myself that I was doing it for *you*, to save you from making a mistake that would last a lifetime. But I know now that I was only lying to myself.'

He braced one hand on the balustrade beside her, making sure to keep some space between them.

'I have never told anyone the things that I told you about my past.' He looked away for a moment, out at the darkness of the water. 'Something about you makes me want to tell you everything. To confide in you and trust you, even though I have spent a lifetime trusting no one. It scared me to death, to be quite honest.'

'Oh, Roman…' she said softly, reaching out her hand to touch him.

He raised his hand, holding her off. 'Wait just another moment. I've been thinking all evening about what I would say when I got here, you see.' He inhaled sharply, felt the adrenaline coursing through him. 'I've spent years—decades—blaming myself for my sister's murder at the hands of a man I trusted. She was shot right in front of me by Alexi, to teach me a lesson.'

Olivia's hands covered her mouth and tears filled her eyes. This was all going wrong, he thought. He hadn't meant to upset her—he just needed her to understand.

He stepped forward, taking her hands in his and kissing her knuckles gently. 'No, please don't cry. Anything but that.' He looked deeply into her eyes. 'I'm telling you this because I want you to understand why I'm such a cold, unlovable bastard. That monster wanted me to see love as a weakness. So he could break me down and make me easier to control. I have unknowingly let that lesson stick to me like tar for the past twenty years. I let that man's actions shape me, even from beyond the grave.'

'You are so brave to have overcome that…' She shook her head. 'To have become what you are now…'

'My success is nothing so long as I am alone,' he said simply, taking a breath and steeling himself for possible rejection.

She was utterly breathtaking, her long fiery hair backlit by the glow of the lights in the garden. The dress she wore was utter perfection in emerald silk, but truly she could have worn rags and he would have found her breathtaking. She was beautiful, it was true. But knowing her as he did now…knowing what lay below that surface beauty… It was infinitely more spectacular.

'I came here to tell you that I love you, Olivia,' he said softly, watching as his words resonated. 'I didn't know how much I needed you until I thought of seeing you on another man's arm. *Any* other man. Of watching you become his wife and have his children… I cannot bear the thought of you marrying anyone… other than me.'

Olivia's heart thumped wildly in her chest as she looked into the solemn, emotion-filled eyes of the man she loved. 'Is that a proposal?' she breathed.

'I hadn't planned on laying it all out like that so quickly,' he said uncertainly. 'I understand if I've done too much. If I've been too cold for you to ever trust me or feel the same way.'

She shook her head, a small smile forming on her lips. 'I trusted you from the moment you offered to take me away with you.'

'Foolish girl.' He smiled, uncertainty still in his eyes.

'But love…?' she said, taking a step closer and running her hand over the lapel of his suit jacket. 'That didn't come until I truly knew you. Knew the man you are underneath all the bravado and the ice.

Then I fell in love with you so deeply it took my breath away.'

He finally took her into his arms. His mouth was hot and demanding on hers as his hands held her tightly against him. His embrace filled her with warmth and strength. When he finally pulled away she groaned with protest, never wanting the moment to end.

'Are you sure you want to marry me? Even though I am no longer a princess?' She let a smile seep into her words as he tipped her back in his arms.

Roman shrugged. 'I suppose it's okay to settle for a simple philanthropist as my wife.' He sighed, sweeping his hands down her sides. 'If you're okay with the fact that *I* don't run an entire kingdom?'

She pretended to consider her options for a long moment, until his hands began to move lower on her hips and he pulled her hard against him in mock warning, with playfulness and a joy that mirrored her own in his eyes.

'I love you, Roman Lazarov,' she said solemnly. 'And nothing would make me happier than becoming your wife.'

The kiss that sealed their engagement was one filled with passion and promises. Olivia sighed with soul-deep contentment as she looked up into the face of the man she loved. The man she had chosen for herself.

Her own destiny.

* * * * *

If you enjoyed
One Night with the Forbidden Princess
you'll love these other stories
by Amanda Cinelli!

Resisting the Sicilian Playboy
The Secret to Marrying Marchesi
Christmas at the Castello

Available now!

#3693 A DEAL FOR THE SICILIAN'S DIAMOND
Conveniently Wed!
by Michelle Smart
Aislin will do anything to secure money for her sick nephew—even pose as billionaire Dante's fiancée at a society wedding. Yet soon their explosive passion rips through the terms of their arrangement, leaving them both hungry for more...

#3694 THE PRINCE'S RUTHLESS WEDDING VOW
by Jane Porter
When Josephine rescues a drowning stranger, she's captivated. Until it's revealed that he's Prince Alexander, heir to the throne of Aargau... Now the threat of scandal means this shy Cinderella must become a royal bride!

#3695 INNOCENT QUEEN BY ROYAL COMMAND
Claimed by a King
by Kelly Hunter
King Augustus is shocked when his country delivers him a courtesan. But Sera's surprising innocence and undisguised yearning for him pushes Augustus's self-control to the limits. Now he won't rest until Sera becomes his queen!

#3696 BILLIONAIRE'S PRISONER IN PARADISE
by Annie West
Finding herself incognito and captive on Alexei's private island, Princess Mina must convince him *she's* his future bride. But after a night in the Greek's bed, there's more at stake than her hidden identity—her heart is at Alexei's mercy, too!

YOU CAN FIND MORE INFORMATION ON UPCOMING HARLEQUIN® TITLES, FREE EXCERPTS AND MORE AT WWW.HARLEQUIN.COM.

HPCNM0119RB

Aislin will do anything to secure money for her sick nephew—even pose as billionaire Dante's fiancée at a society wedding. Yet soon their explosive passion rips through the terms of their arrangement, leaving them both hungry for more…

Read on for a sneak preview of Michelle Smart's next story,
The Sicilian's Bought Cinderella.

"But…" Aislin couldn't form anything more than that one syllable. Dante's offer had thrown her completely.

His smile was rueful. "My offer is simple, *dolcezza.* You come to the wedding with me and I give you a million euros."

He pronounced it *"seemple,"* a quirk she would have found endearing if her brain hadn't frozen into a stunned snowball.

"You want to pay me to come to a wedding with you?"

"Si." He unfolded his arms and spread his hands. "The money will be yours. You can give as much or as little of it to your sister."

It took a huge amount of effort to keep her voice steady. "But you must have a heap of women you could take and not have to pay them for it."

"None of them are suitable."

"What does that mean?"

"I need to make an impression on someone and having you on my arm will assist in that."

"A million dollars for one afternoon?"

"I never said it would be for an afternoon. The celebrations will take place over the coming weekend."

She tugged at her ponytail. "Weekend?"

"Aislin, the groom is one of Sicily's richest men. It is a necessity that his wedding be the biggest and flashiest it can be."

She almost laughed at the deadpan way he explained it.

She didn't need to ask who the richest man in Sicily was.

"If I'm going to accept your offer, what else do I need to know?"

"Nothing… Apart from that I will be introducing you as my fiancée."

"What?" Aislin winced at the squeakiness of her tone.

"I require you to play the role of my fiancée." His grin was wide with just a touch of ruefulness. The deadened, shocked look that had rung from his eyes only a few minutes before had gone. Now they sparkled with life, and it was almost hypnotizing.

She blinked the effect away.

"Why do you need a fiancée?"

"Because the father of the bride thinks going into business with me will damage his reputation."

"How?"

"I will go through the reasons once I have your agreement on the matter. I appreciate it is a lot to take in so I'm going to leave you to sleep on it. You can give me your answer in the morning. If you're in agreement then I shall take you home with me and give you more details. We will have a few days to get to know each other and work on putting on a convincing act."

"And if I say no?"

He shrugged. "If you say no, then no million euros."

Don't miss
The Sicilian's Bought Cinderella,
available February 2019 wherever
Harlequin Presents® books and ebooks are sold.

www.Harlequin.com

HARLEQUIN *Presents*®

**Coming next month—escape with this
spellbinding royal duo!**

**Read *The Prince's Scandalous Wedding Vow*, Jane Porter's
deeply emotional royal romance. Innocent Josephine finds
it impossible to ignore her instant connection to mysterious
Alexander—but will his royal secret change everything?**

When Josephine rescues a drowning stranger,
she's captivated. Until it's revealed he's Prince Alexander,
heir to the throne of Aargau... Now the threat of scandal
means this shy Cinderella must become a royal bride!

**Discover *Innocent Queen by Royal Command*,
part of Kelly Hunter's sinful and sexy Claimed by a King
miniseries. His royal duty must come before anything,
but will King Augustus be able to resist temptation?**

King Augustus is shocked when his country
delivers him a courtesan. But Sera's surprising innocence
and undisguised yearning for him pushes Augustus's
self-control to the limits. Now he won't rest until
Sera becomes his queen!

Available February 2019

HPBPA0119R